THE DEVIL AND DR TUBEROSE

THE DEVIL
AND DR TUBEROSE

Scottish Short Stories
1991

INTRODUCTION BY
Brian McCabe

HarperCollins
An Imprint of HarperCollins*Publishers*

First published in 1991
by HarperCollins Publishers,
77–85 Fulham Palace Road,
Hammersmith, London w6 8jb

9 8 7 6 5 4 3 2 1

The Publisher acknowledges the financial assistance of the
Scottish Arts Council in the publication of this volume.

A catalogue record for this book is available from
the British Library

ISBN 0 00 223860 8 (hb)
0 00 223861 6 (pb)

Photoset in Linotron Baskerville by
Rowland Phototypesetting Ltd
Bury St Edmunds, Suffolk
Printed and bound in Great Britain by
HarperCollins Book Manufacturing, Glasgow

CONTENTS

CONTENTS

INTRODUCTION

Someone, somewhere, once said to me that they wouldn't submit one of their short stories to *Scottish Short Stories*, despite my advice that they should do so, because the story was 'too experimental'. The implication was that this annual series of anthologies was too 'safe', too unadventurous to accept work which would be considered 'experimental'. I think this year's volume might make him less reluctant to invest in the stamps, though it depends what is meant by 'experimental'. Genuinely experimental work, by which I mean work which attempts to use language innovatively, or does something fresh with narrative, or adds something new to our understanding of what the short story is, is I believe quite rare. More common is experimental writing which is poor writing dressed up to look and sound strange and different, or writing which betrays an ignorance of what fiction, essentially, is.

The fact is, only a small part of this year's submission could be classed as 'experimental' in either the good or the bad sense of that unfortunate term, and most of those fell into the latter category: they were not stories, but illustrations of abstract ideas, or ways of raising sociological issues, or expressions of the writer's presumably heartfelt emotions. These writers forget that the materials of the fiction writer are the humblest, as Flannery O'Connor, one of the short story's finest practitioners, went out of her way to make plain on more than one occasion:

> Fiction operates through the senses, and I think one rea-
> son that people find it so difficult to write stories is that
> they forget how much time and patience is required to
> convince through the senses. No reader who doesn't
> actually experience, who isn't made to feel, the story is

going to believe anything the fiction writer merely tells him. The first and most obvious characteristic of fiction is that it deals with reality through what can be seen, heard, smelt, tasted and touched.

Janice Galloway's 'The Chlorine Bath' seems 'experimental' in that at first sight it seems to leave a great deal unexplained, but we realize that what is given is enough. What we are given is, in effect, an experience in close-up. It does not matter whether we are in the locked ward of a mental hospital or somewhere else. What matters is the foreground of the experience, and the narrator's apprehensions of humiliation. A subjective item, you may think, but Janice Galloway knows that to convey this she must provide us with enough specific, sensory detail to take us into that strangely threatening environment and under that woman's skin.

One heartening aspect of this year's submission for me was the interest in spoken language evident in many of the stories. More writers are interested in rendering dialect accurately, for example, whether it be in the use of a central narrative voice, as in William Oliphant's 'Bearsden Bagatelle' and Christina Mills's 'The Wife at Number Seven', or in the speech of the characters, as in 'Pass the Parcel', in which Gordon Burnside uses phonetics to catch the pronunciation and the speech patterns of a specifically Dundee dialect. Less overtly concerned with dialect, but focusing just as emphatically on narrative voice, is Allan Mitchell Fowlie's chilling 'Scum of the Earth'.

The use of a speaker and the attempt to render dialect accurately have long been central concerns in Scottish poetry and perhaps the work of James Kelman and the renewal of interest in the work of James Hogg has done something to encourage fiction writers to explore this territory as well. In any case, this seems to me to be a very healthy development. There is, of course, the possibility of wallowing in the localized, a kind of linguistic parochialism. The universal mustn't get lost in the particular, but be revealed in it. To ignore the patterns of speech which surround us in Scotland is to run the risk of jettisoning the social fabric from which it springs, and this is something Flannery O'Connor also emphasized in her essay 'Writing Short Stories':

> You can't say anything meaningful about the mystery of a personality unless you put that personality in a believable and significant social context. And the best way to do this is through the character's own language.

It is customary to say a word or two about the procedure of selection. Though Deirdre Chapman, Jonathan Warner and myself are not by nature intransigent people, the selection was, I suppose, as difficult as usual. I had come to the meeting with the foolishly optimistic belief that we would probably be in unanimous agreement about at least half a dozen of the stories submitted. In fact, all three of us were definite about only one story, but there were many more which had won over two of the three judges. Special pleas were made and opinions were swayed, stories at first excluded were reread, reconsidered and sometimes readmitted. Even so I am sure that all three editors saw at least one of their personal favourites squeezed out. The recently introduced policy of passing the stories to the editors without the names of the authors was continued, and again the result is a democratic collection of stories by well-known writers, writers gaining recognition and writers published here for the first time.

BRIAN MCCABE

SCOTTISH
SHORT STORIES

THE DEVIL AND DR TUBEROSE
John Herdman

Dr Marcus Tuberose was being victimized. Whether it was because he had a poetic temperament, or because of his present difficult domestic circumstances, or because of the machinations of Dr Philip Pluckrose, his rival and enemy, or whether all these factors were fatally combining to discredit and disadvantage him, was not yet clear. An artistic sensibility, he well knew, was not a recommendation in the world of academic departmental politics; rather it was a focus of jealousy, suspicion and mistrust. Dr Tuberose did not flaunt his superiority in the very least; but neither, on the other hand, did he attempt hypocritically to conceal it. He knew his worth, and he knew that some day that worth would be recognized. But his openness in this respect did put him at a disadvantage, he was well aware of that. He did not conceal that from himself, not at all.

The fact that he had recently been deserted by his wife, Malitia, did not help either. The break-up of a marriage might no longer in itself be a social embarrassment, but in this case the circumstances, the particular and special circumstances . . . Dr Tuberose was not unconscious of the fact that there were people who did not scruple to laugh at him behind his back. People were like that, and academics in particular were like that. Dr Tuberose knew that he had not always made himself popular. He spoke his mind when it would be against his conscience to keep silent, and that was not a worldly-wise thing to do. But he thanked God that worldly wisdom had never been a part of his make-up. He was also not adept at currying favour in high places, unlike certain successful departmental politicians he could think of. It was amazing, he always thought, how intelligent people were so easily taken in by flattery. But then vanity was a powerful force, a more

3

powerful force than intelligence, or disinterested commitment, a much stronger force than honesty or intellectual integrity . . . that was the way the world was, the way it had always been.

Ever since it had become known that Professor McSpale was to spend the coming academic year at the University of Delaware, a certain sentence had kept revolving and repeating itself in Dr Tuberose's head. He had not exactly composed it, it had come, as it were, unbidden and without his full consent. These things happened to people of a poetic sensibility, of an intuitive temperament, they were not altogether under conscious control. 'Marcus Aurelius Tuberose MA B. Litt PhD, has been appointed Acting Head of the Department of English Literature for the academic year 1988–89.' That was the little sentence, or jingle. It was silly, he knew – he was even a little ashamed of it, deep down. But, after all, the message which it contained communicated an essential truth. The formal recognition which that sentence would represent, should it ever emerge into outer reality, would be no more than he deserved. He did not expect it or ask for it, he disdained to canvas it or tout for it or flatter for it, but he was too honest to hide from himself the simple fact that he deserved it. Not that he wanted it, no, but simply that he deserved it.

A month ago it had seemed to him that it was really going to happen. Things were looking good, he felt, he was not blind to the impression that there were certain factors in his favour, certain realities which it would be foolish to ignore, unrealistic, in a sense, to disregard . . . Then had come the day of the departmental meeting. Dr Tuberose had arrived early, but Philip Pluckrose was there before him, and so, strange to say, was Professor McSpale. Dr Tuberose did not like the smell of that. They were huddled deep in conversation when he entered, McSpale expatiating assertively but in low, almost conspiratorial tones, Pluckrose nodding vehemently, but with a look of fawning obsequiousness that was quite revolting. When Tuberose entered the room they ceased their confabulations quite suddenly, even blatantly, as if scorning to conceal the truth that they had been saying things that were not for

4

his ears, things that were almost certainly to his direct disadvantage.

The decision on the appointment of the Acting Head of the Department was deferred until the next meeting. Tuberose did not like that, it was clear to him that it meant that whatever understanding was being worked out between McSpale and Pluckrose required time to be brought to fruition, that it was unscrupulously being given time, and that time was therefore on the side of his enemies. During the course of that afternoon, he was frequently aware of Professor McSpale directing at him, from under his coarse, tangled, greying eyebrows, a quite peculiar look. It was a look that, thinking about it afterwards, he found it very hard to analyse. It was a look of scorn, perhaps, of hard, cold scorn, and there was something insolently defiant about it, something altogether blatant. It seemed to say that power was going to be exercised, directly and shamelessly, that justice and right were going to be disregarded, trampled upon, set altogether at nought, that this was wrong, yes, certainly, but it was going to happen all the same, and there was nothing whatever that Dr Tuberose could do about it, not this time. This, Tuberose realized, was the price of integrity, this was the cost of speaking one's mind.

Ever since that meeting the attitude of condescending friendliness which Philip Pluckrose customarily adopted towards him had become more odiously bland, and at the same time more unconcealedly tinctured with genial contempt. On one occasion he had even had the effrontery to pretend to commiserate with Tuberose about his domestic misfortune. 'You'll have to come and have a meal with Polly and I,' he had fawned with his customary grammatical insensibility, 'and if there is anything we can do to help, Marcus, you know we're always at the end of the phone . . .' – and so on and so on. It would be embarrassing to record all the banal, gloating hypocrisies that oozed from his lips and hung heavily in the air like halitosis.

But Dr Tuberose's nature was not of the kind that lies down meekly under persecution. He had, of course, the clean bright shield of conscious integrity with which to defend himself, but he had something else too, something more tellingly substantial – an eloquent expression of his worth that would be hard for anyone simply to ignore, even the hardened careerists of the department, to whom intellectual distinction was apparently such a contemptible irrelevance in the primitive struggle for place, power and personal advantage. This secret weapon was his new lecture course on the 'Romantic Imagination', which was to form the nucleus, the matrix, of his projected work on this well-worn topic. Already, in spite of himself, Dr Tuberose could hear phantom phrases from future critical commentaries on this embryonic work of genius flitting restlessly about his brain: 'allusive, learned, lucid and perspicacious'; 'the daring taxonomies of Tuberose'; 'as Tuberose has seminally suggested'; and so on and so forth.

Everything, however, depended on the success of the lecture course, really everything. Dr Tuberose was now in such a position and of such an age that if he didn't go up, he could only go down – or even out. Things being as they were in the academic world, it was either promotion or early retirement, Tuberose knew that. Since the most recent departmental meeting he was aware, too, that the odds were stacked heavily against him. But the lecture course might yet change all that. There were some things that simply couldn't be disregarded, even by the English Department – one had to believe that, or life could hold no meaning.

In the early hours of the morning on which he was to deliver his first lecture in the series, Dr Tuberose awoke in his lonely bed moaning and groaning from a most appalling nightmare . . .

Entering through the sliding doors of the main arts building of the University, his lecture notes in his briefcase, he found himself, without surprise, in the chamber of the House of Commons. A vast crowd composed of students, newspaper correspondents, internationally famous critics, and even a few well-known movie stars, was wedged closely in the benches and thronging eagerly in the aisles, jostling for position, manifesting every symptom of impatient excitement, awaiting in breathless anticipation some crucial public announcement. As the bewildered Tuberose mingled with the throng, an official in the shape of a

Himalayan bear advanced towards the Speaker's chair, followed by Professor McSpale in the garb of the Lord Chancellor. The Himalayan bear banged three times on the ground with his ceremonial staff and called for silence. Professor McSpale instantly picked out Tuberose among the seething press and fixed on him, for a terrible moment, a baleful eye flashing with a most hellishly malignant lustre. Then he averted his gaze and, drawing from among the folds of his gown a slip of paper, read out in clear and ringing tones: 'Philip Endymion Pluckrose MA D. Phil, has been appointed Acting Head of the Department of English Literature for the academic year 1988–89.'

A wild cheer rose up, and instantly every eye was turned upon Dr Tuberose with open, wicked mockery, while raucous laughter burst out and jeers, whistles and catcalls smote upon his ears. He dropped his head in shame and struggled to leave, but no one would let him pass; instead they shoved and shouldered him provocatively while heaping upon him vague but deadly insults. Then Professor McSpale pointed to him with his long, lank, skinny finger, slapped the Himalayan bear on the rump and shouted, 'Go get him, Spielberg!' The crowd instantly parted, and the bear charged down the aisle towards Dr Tuberose with slavering fangs – there was nowhere for him to flee. Its teeth were not a hair's-breadth from his throat . . .

The unhappy scholar awoke. In pitiable condition, Dr Tuberose tossed and turned hopelessly for the remainder of that night, as fragments of his lecture, the announcement by Professor McSpale, the superior smile of Pluckrose, and the teeth of the Himalayan bear mingled and coalesced in the fevered jumble of his imagination.

It may be imagined that Dr Tuberose entered the lecture hall considerably unnerved. He was made of stern stuff, however; Marcus Aurelius Tuberose was not a man of jelly and, in spite of every setback, he remained quietly but ruthlessly determined to do himself justice, to acquit himself with honour, to put all his cards squarely on the table, to show up Pluckrose for what he was. In this first lecture he was plunging right into the very heart of the matter, addressing Coleridge's distinction between Fancy and Imagination. As he warmed to his subject he began to be stirred and even exalted by his own eloquence, and soon he was confident that he had his audience

7

eating out of the palm of his hand. The tables were turned, Pluckrose was a dead letter – even in the impetuous onrush of his discourse that consciousness was shining at the back of Tuberose's mind. And then a terrible thing happened.

'We have, above all, to ask ourselves,' Dr Tuberose was saying as he reached what he thought of as the high point of his lecture, 'what exactly Coleridge meant by "Imagination". We have to be clear about this before we can proceed any further. Did he mean by imagination a permanent, universal faculty of the human mind, equally possessed by all? Or did he mean by it what we nowadays usually understand the term to mean, namely a mere image-forming capacity, an ability to image to ourselves facts and possibilities and potentialities outside immediate reality, a capacity which different people possess in differing and variable degrees? Do we all possess imagination in the same way in which we all possess two arms and two legs?'

Dr Tuberose paused impressively and looked around at his audience. He was about to continue when he noticed a hand raised about three-quarters of the way up the lecture hall, to his right, near a side-entrance. To his irritation, and with a certain sinking of the heart, he saw that it belonged to an unhealthy-looking young man in a wheelchair, the lower moiety of whose person was concealed by a travelling-rug.

'Yes?' he snapped impatiently, in a way which he hoped indicated that interruptions were not scheduled for this lecture course.

'Excuse me,' came back at him the weak, but at the same time assertive, tones of the student in the wheelchair, 'but it is not true that we all possess two arms and two legs.'

Dr Tuberose frowned and traversed the rostrum once or twice, looking at his feet.

'Let me rephrase that,' he resumed. 'Do we all possess imagination in the same way in which we all possess a head?' He paused again. 'Or am I once again assuming too much? Is there anyone here without a head?'

This sally was met with a horrified, stunned silence.

'So,' said Dr Tuberose complacently, 'we all have heads.' He paused yet again. 'But perhaps there is among us some smart-arse with *two* heads, who would like to exploit his – or, I had no doubt better add, her – misfortune in order to score a debating point off me?'

At this, signs of disorder began to manifest themselves in the lecture hall: there was some laughter of a nervous kind, but also more ominous stirrings and mutterings. Dr Tuberose raised his voice.

'I can see that I shall have to make a diversion, in order to attempt to establish the distinction between essence and accident. The essence of a thing refers to that which it is in itself, its inner, universal condition; its accidents refer to that which has befallen it accidentally, that, in other words, which has *happened* to it. The essence of a thing is undisturbed by its accidents.'

'It wasn't an accident!' shouted the student in the wheel-chair, 'I was born without legs!'

'You misunderstand me!' yelled back Dr Tuberose. 'You misunderstand me deliberately and maliciously! That you were born without legs is an accident, essentially you have legs! I will not be provoked! I will not be persecuted!'

Scarcely aware of what he was doing, shaking with fury but also close to tears, he began gathering up his papers and stuffing them into his briefcase. There was a vague conscious-ness in him that he was crossing some kind of Rubicon, that he was recklessly hurling himself forward into a region whence there is no return, but he did not care, the ardour and impetu-osity of his temperament carried him onwards and could not be withstood; and furthermore he was right, right beyond a shadow of doubting, persecuted and provoked and buffeted by the tempests of ill-fortune, but right, right, right . . . The students were too shocked to move or speak, they sat on in wide-eyed amazement, although a few were tentatively stand-ing up, it was hard to say why. Dr Tuberose tore out of the lecture hall, made straight for the staff toilet and plunged his head into a basin of cold water.

He just could not account for this unprovoked attack. He was aware that he was liberal even to a fault, entirely confident that his record was irreproachable. He had always, as it happened, had particularly compassionate feelings and views about the treatment of the limbless. Had he not, as a matter of fact, been directly responsible, through his forceful eloquence at a crucial meeting of the University Council, for the installation of ramps and electrically-operated sliding doors throughout the lecture block – was it not through his caring vigilance that the very ramp existed by which his assailant had ascended to his commanding position above Dr Tuberose? And was this his reward? More, had he not agitated, unsuccessfully it was true but sincerely, for the removal from the University Library of all shelves higher than three feet from the ground? And how was he now rewarded?

But when at length he emerged from the toilet, everything became instantly and chillingly clear. Little groups of students from his truncated lecture were standing around in animated conversation; there was a general buzz of excited gossip and speculation; there was seriousness and there was laughter; there was a little hilarity but perhaps a great deal more righteous indignation. Around the student in the wheelchair a particularly large and vocal group had gathered, and among them, with a lunge of panic, a stab of recognition and at the same time a detached, ironical insight, a sigh of inevitability, he identified the little Mephistophilean beard and the brown corduroy jacket of Philip Endymion Pluckrose. Tuberose realized now, with a calm certainty, that all this had been planned long ago. A student had been suborned, his lecture course deliberately sabotaged, and it was, of course, precisely this that McSpale had been plotting with Pluckrose on the afternoon of the departmental meeting.

Tuberose gazed at his enemy with a disgust too deep for words. Pluckrose always looked to him as if he were in disguise, like a spy in a bad comedy film of the fifties. The ascetic cut of his meagre, jet-black hair suggested a renegade monk of the Renaissance, despatched on some obscure and dubious mission to a distant court – an aspiring poisoner, perhaps – while his black trimmed beard gave the impression of being hooked over his ears. The truth, thought Tuberose, was that Pluckrose *was* in disguise, hiding his malice and hopeless mediocrity, poisoning the minds of the young, poisoning the wells of truth, poisoning them all against Tuberose, the righteous one, the disinterested one, the man of integrity. Pluckrose the poisoner.

There had to be a confrontation, Tuberose knew that, but not yet. Now was not the time. The students were incensed, they had been stirred up against him, bought by Pluckrose, and he could hope for no justice there. But tonight he would speak out – yes, tonight, at Cowperthwaite's party. Everybody in the department would be there, everybody who counted, anyway. McSpale, on the other hand, he knew, had been obliged to refuse the invitation, or at least had made some excuse, and that was greatly in the favour of Dr Tuberose. Without McSpale, Pluckrose was nothing, a mere paper tiger, a hand puppet from which the hand had been withdrawn, essentially just a limp rag. In fact, to call Pluckrose a limp rag was to flatter him.

When Tuberose had said what he had to say, Pluckrose would be finished, it would be totally out of the question that he could become Acting Head of Department, he would be obliged instead to apply for early retirement, and he would be lucky if he got that, very lucky indeed. In fact he would be much more likely to be up before the University disciplinary committee, a fate normally reserved for only the most hopeless drunks, and he might even have to leave the country. And then, of course, Tuberose would come into his own. His worth would be recognized, his disinterested and fearless exposure of Pluckrose would be widely discussed and favourably assessed, integrity would win through, truth would prevail and poetic sensibility be vindicated, he would be appointed Acting Head of Department, the idea of a personal Chair would be mooted, his book on the Romantic Imagination would be praised by George Steiner, he would succeed McSpale, and so on and so forth . . .

Dr Tuberose was known not to be a heavy drinker, and had he over-indulged himself on the occasion of the Cowperthwaites' party it would have been quite out of character. On the other hand, a man of his delicate frame, and of a constitution unaccustomed to alcohol, might, I suppose, have been more affected than another by a little Dutch courage. At the time of his arrival at the party those present all agreed that Dr

Tuberose did not really appear to be drunk. It is more likely that his susceptible and excitable temperament was agitated by his horribly disturbed night and by the most unfortunate incident which had interrupted so inauspiciously the first in his series of lectures. He had, besides, been under considerable strain for some time past as a result of his unfortunate domestic circumstances.

Everybody enjoyed the little gatherings given once or twice a year by Cowperthwaite and his lovely wife, Aminta. Cowperthwaite was a remarkable man. His favourite word was 'teleological', though he was pretty keen also on 'ontological', 'epistemological' and 'taxonomy'. He was always calling his children 'darling' and his wife 'sweetheart', and sometimes he would even address the family dog, Demiurge, as 'darling'. Aminta was not quite as intelligent as her husband, though not, of course, by any means unintelligent. Perhaps for this reason, she was a stabilizing influence on the wilder flights of Cowperthwaite's speculative conjectures. She spoke to him habitually in a teasing tone which conveyed that for all his little weaknesses there was really no one in the world quite so wonderful as he. That is not to say that he was not at times an embarrassment to her: when, on one dire occasion that evening, he spoke of the 'Heraclitean flux', her reaction was such as to suggest that she had mistaken that ontological phenomenon for a form of dysentery.

Demiurge, who is to play a not unimportant part in this tale of truth, was a cross between a spaniel and a corgi, something that can't possibly be imagined until it has been seen. As to his name, he was the victim of some obscure academic joke, a fate which, along with his appearance, probably contributed to his habitual look of shame, as if he were the author of some vile mess on the carpet which was perpetually the subject of discussion. Though known familiarly in the household as 'Demmy', he seemed to know that this was merely a diminutive, and to live in constant fear that the guilty secret of his full name would be revealed to visitors; as, indeed, it often was, thanks to his master's keenness to tell the story attached to the name, which displayed his genial intelligence to especial advantage.

I wish I could describe the wit and urbanity and the relaxed intellectual authority which marked the tone of that memorable evening: the talk of contemporary film, of child abuse, of advanced social theory, of construction and deconstruction, of Adorno and Jürgen Habermas, of 'the Frenchman Derrida' (whose name I personally would have pronounced 'Dereeda', but whom all of that company, and certainly correctly, called 'Derry Dah'); and at the same time the common touch, the homely aspersions on the Thatcher Government, the substitution of the word 'Jockish' for 'Scottish', and other little foibles to which it would be unpardonably bad taste to draw attention; and then the sense almost of an extended family, united in benignity and complacency of feeling, in the best sense – all this I would love to be able to depict. But my talents are not equal to the task – I lack the qualifications. Certain it is that anyone who had strayed by chance among those excellent people, lacking a doctorate or at the absolute minimum a very good honours degree, would have felt diffident and tongue-tied in the extreme; indeed even with these recommendations, but lacking the easy fluency which knows how to deploy difficult and complex, obscure and advanced ideas with geniality and deceptive simplicity and unostentatious control, such a person might have felt distinctly inferior and out of place.

The delightful atmosphere which I have just haltingly attempted to convey was already well established when Dr Tuberose made his entry. He was unaccompanied, embarrassingly so, for when his wife had left him five months previously it had soon emerged that she was living with a Chinese waiter in Burntisland. Cowperthwaite and Aminta, in fact, had invited him partly out of sympathy and fellow-feeling, for Adrian, their seventeen-year-old son, was living with another Chinese waiter in Tollcross. When Dr Tuberose came in they were all discussing Rudolf Steiner play-groups. As Tuberose advanced into the room with an intent but somehow abstracted look on his sensitive little face, a knowing, almost scornful little smile playing about the corners of his mouth, and an exalted expressiveness in his light grey eyes, the guests turned towards him with genial, welcoming expansiveness.

Dr Tuberose nodded vaguely at his acquaintances, his eyes flickering over the company, searching for Pluckrose. At that moment, an amazing incident occurred.

Demiurge, who up till then had been dozing comfortably beside the fire, having decided that the conversation, fascinating though it doubtless was, was way above his head, now suddenly sat up, the hair rising along his back, and staring at Tuberose with every sign of venomous hostility, growled at him in the most menacing manner, and even started to yap in a pitch of hellish stridency, advancing towards Tuberose and then backing away again as if uncertain whether the situation called for attack or defence. Tuberose, quite unnerved, retreated against a sideboard. Cowperthwaite, in complete consternation, abandoned the drinks he had been pouring and hastened over, crying, 'Demmy! Demmy! What is it, darling? You know Uncle Marcus! It's only Uncle Marcus, Demmy, he won't hurt you, sweetheart!'

Demiurge, however, was not to be pacified so easily. He was now yapping furiously and pertinaciously, and as it were with a growing confidence in the justice of his cause; Dr Tuberose had retreated within a protective ring of guests, utterly taken aback but conscious of a dawning recognition that something was afoot, that there was more here than met the eye. Sterner measures were clearly required, and now Cowperthwaite rapped out, 'Demiurge!' in a tone of warning, and with a rising emphasis on the final syllable.

The uttering of this shameful name had an instantaneous effect on the poor animal. With an appearance of great fright he shot off with his tail between his legs and slumped abjectly on the hearthrug: it was really impossible not to feel sorry for him. He now lay unmoving with his head between his paws, and soon commenced making ostentatious snuffling noises and settling his lips, as if he had never had any other thought in his head but to prepare for sleep. It was all a show, however. Shortly, he began once more to cast furtive glances at Dr Tuberose, and once the commotion had died down a little and he was no longer an object of scrutiny, he kept following 'Uncle Marcus' with his eyes, with an unfathomable gaze that spoke volumes, but in some unknown tongue.

The party had no sooner settled back into normality than the telephone rang. Cowperthwaite left the room to answer it, and after a brief absence returned and called over to Aminta, 'That was Phil Pluckrose, sweetheart. He sends his apologies, they won't be coming. It seems McSpale needed to see him very urgently about something.' Dr Tuberose was at this moment in conversation with a psychiatrist whom he had always known simply as 'Justin's Daddy'. Justin's Daddy had a club foot, for which reason he had been called 'Dr Goebbels' at school, which just goes to show how cruel children can be; a few unpleasant people still referred to him by that name, though not of course in his hearing. Justin's Daddy, who had met Dr Tuberose socially on two or three previous occasions, had suddenly become interested in him when, a few minutes previously, he had overheard him say to Cowperthwaite, 'Did you notice how McSpale kept staring at me during the department meeting? There was an awful depth and malignancy in his eye . . .' ('Oh, dear,' Aminta had interrupted with sweet concern, 'has he got cancer?') Now, when the news about Pluckrose was announced, Dr Tuberose broke off in mid-sentence and his poetic face at once took on a horrified, haunted, harried look, a look which caused Justin's Daddy to observe him with an almost professional concern. But no one else noticed.

The company was artistically dispersed all round the room, chatting expansively. The subject of conversation was the reading given the previous Saturday evening by the poet Brechin of his epic work, *The Old Dying Sheep*.

'I take it that it is intended as an allegory of the fate of the artist in a materialistic society,' observed Robin Dross-Jones, who wrote a very highly regarded newspaper column, 'Vermicular Viewpoint'.

'Yes, but the symbolism can be understood at a number of different levels,' responded Cowperthwaite sagaciously. 'We could also, for instance, assume the old dying sheep to be Scotland.'

'And surely there's a rather impudent, tongue-in-cheek allusion to the motif of the young dying god?' suggested someone else.

'Indeed,' said Cowperthwaite, 'why not? The image means all of these things, of course, and at the same time none of them. Finally, perhaps, it's about himself that Brechin is speaking,' he closed, magisterially. There was a great deal of affirmatory grunting and vehement nodding of heads.

'Brechin was completely legless last time I saw him,' remarked Robin Dross-Jones.

'Legless?' cried Dr Tuberose suddenly, in terrible agitation. 'Did you say legless?'

The creator of 'Vermicular Viewpoint' stared at him. 'Yes, legless,' he replied. 'You know . . . drunk.'

'Ah,' said Dr Tuberose, relieved, but still suspicious.

'But that was after his mother's funeral, dear,' said Florrie Dross-Jones.

'My mother was always belittling me,' put in Dr Tuberose wildly, 'devaluing me, casting aspersions on me! "I'm sorry for your wife," she would say, "if you ever get one." I always remember that, I can never forget it! What a thing to say to a child: "I'm sorry for your wife, if you ever get one."'

'Oh, dear,' said Aminta, faintly.

'And now, you see,' continued Dr Tuberose relentlessly, 'she is living with a Chinese waiter in . . . in . . . Burntisland. Not that I have anything against the Chinese, who are an industrious little people. The man has legs, so far as I am aware, and not by accident. Yes, he has legs, and everything else that he needs to betray me!' He looked around the room and was vaguely aware of the terrible embarrassment and consternation which he was causing. 'I'm sorry,' he said, and passed his hand over his eyes. 'This is the price I have to pay for having the sensibility of a poet.'

No one said anything. After a quite long and very awkward silence, they all, as if by a prearranged signal, began talking about where they had been and what they had been doing when Kennedy was assassinated.

'I was still at school,' said Aminta, and for some reason this was greeted with howls of urbane laughter. 'I can't remember what I was doing – I expect I was doing my sums.'

'I think I was cutting my toenails,' said Dr Tuberose. 'It's a strange thing, you know, but I have rather coarse feet. My hands are sensitive and artistic, but my feet are rather solid, coarse and peasant-like.'

Demiurge, who had been keeping his own counsel for some time, now growled most threateningly at Dr Tuberose. Cowperthwaite at once went over to the dog and tried to quieten him.

'Come on, Urgie-Purgie, who loves his daddy?' he coaxed gently.

But whoever loved his daddy, it didn't appear to be Urgie-Purgie. He sat up, staring at Dr Tuberose, and began once more to yap in a frightened but challenging and even provocative tone. Dr Tuberose sprang to his feet in a dawning epiphany: he had just understood something. This was not Demiurge. This was not the Demiurge he knew, not the dog whose long floppy ears he had fondled when he was a puppy, no, no, no: this was, on the contrary, Philip Endymion Pluckrose, MA D. Phil!

This insight did not represent quite such a remarkable imaginative leap on the part of Dr Tuberose as might at first appear. For, you see, earlier that afternoon, he had realized, quite suddenly, that Pluckrose was the devil. The truth had dawned on him after he had been struck outside the lecture hall by how Mephistophilean, even Luciferean, was Pluckrose's little black beard: it flashed on him then that Pluckrose was not just metaphorically but literally in disguise, that he was in fact the devil! As he had mulled over his dream of the previous night, it had become quite clear to Dr Tuberose that the official in the form of a Himalayan bear whom McSpale had set on him could only be Pluckrose, that is, the devil, in another guise. McSpale was God the Father, or more strictly (since Dr Tuberose was a man of sophisticated literary sensibility) he was a symbolic projection of God the Father; and he was testing Dr Tuberose by giving Satan power over him for a season, as he had done many years before with his servant Job. How perfectly it all fitted into place! How ever had he failed to see it before! He was being tested and proved like gold, and he must not be found wanting. And now Pluckrose the devil had come to him in yet another guise, in the form of Demiurge the dog, and he must stand up to him and confront him boldly.

Dr Tuberose was now completely fearless. He advanced towards Demiurge with his left hand in his trouser pocket, a glass of wine in the other sensitive instrument, his head slightly on one side in an almost effeminate attitude, and a complacent, knowing smirk on his small, refined features.

'Do you imagine that I am stupid, Pluckrose?' he commenced quietly, utterly in control of himself. The dog stopped yapping and stared in astonishment. 'Do you think you can fool *me*? You can appear as a dog or a Himalayan bear or as King Kong, if you choose, it's entirely up to you. You are being used, Pluckrose, don't you realize that? You are no more than an instrument. Every dog has his day, and you have had yours. The future is mine. Justice will prevail, truth will prevail. You are yesterday's man, Pluckrose. In fact, if you only knew it, you were yesterday's man yesterday. I know who you are. But perhaps you don't know who McSpale is . . . I shall be Acting Head of Department! It has been decided and ordained!'

Dr Tuberose's calm tone had been giving way during the course of this harangue to one of inspired, prophetic conviction, and now this in its turn was converted into righteous fury. Dr Tuberose cast his glass to the floor, dropped to his knees and faced Demiurge nose to nose.

'Mongrel trash!' he cried impetuously. 'I'll cut off your legs, you mongrel trash! Dog of hell!'

The ruin of a noble mind is always pitiful; but this was a terrible reversal to behold, the man in the role of the beast. Demiurge backed away from the raging madman, howling with terror. But now the Cowperthwaites' twelve-year-old daughter, who had been standing listening by the door, rushed forward fearlessly, gathered up Demiurge in her arms, and ran out with him, crying, 'Never mind, Demmy! Never mind, my poor little Semi-semi-demiurge! Pay no attention to the silly, bad man!'

Cowperthwaite had already gone into a huddle with Justin's Daddy; they were talking eagerly, excitedly but in hushed tones. Dr Tuberose found himself sitting bemusedly on a three-legged stool, in calm of mind, all passion spent. Florrie Dross-Jones had given him a Perrier water, which she said was very good for the digestion. Fragments of conversation reached Dr Tuberose from the group clustering around Justin's Daddy over by the door.

'I can arrange for him to be admitted tonight . . .'

'We'd better start phoning for a taxi right away, it'll take ages on a Friday night . . .'

'It's all right, we've ordered one already, you can take that, we can wait . . .'

'Poor man!'

'Phil Pluckrose will have to take over his lecture course.'

'Out of the question with all his departmental responsibilities.'

'That's not till next year. Phil's the only one . . .'

'Oh, no, Angela Mulhearn could do it very competently. It's well within her field of interest.'

'Should we let Malitia know, do you think?'

'Good God, no!'

'Better phone his GP, perhaps. I think it's Gebbie.'

'No, no, there's no problem there, he can be taken in tonight.'

'No, no, I cannot be taken in!' cried Dr Tuberose suddenly. 'You can take me in, if you understand me, but I cannot be taken in. I know a hawk from a handsaw.'

'Don't worry, Marcus, Justin's Daddy is going to take you home. He'll give you something to make you sleep, you'll be fine in the morning.'

'I see, you want me to go with Dr Goebbels here? Well, that's all right! Legs eleven – bingo! And not by accident. Yes, the legs of a Chinese waiter, with a club foot at one end and betrayal at the other!'

'It's funny, you very seldom see a club foot nowadays,' said Aminta, in the general confusion quite forgetting about Justin's Daddy. Then she remembered. 'Oh, dear! But it's wonderful what they can do nowadays,' she added vaguely.

The door-bell rang. 'That's the taxi!' everybody shouted at once.

'I'll let the driver know you're coming,' said Robin Dross-Jones eagerly, and rushed down the stairs.

Dr Goebbels took Dr Tuberose gently but very firmly by the elbow and steered him towards the front door; he let himself be taken, offering no resistance. Everyone was crowding around him with looks and words of sympathy and concern, but Dr Tuberose was no longer in need of sympathy or concern, for he had understood it all. Everything had suddenly become crystal clear to him, and though it would be impossible to put into words the full depth and comprehensiveness of his understanding, there was no mistaking its reality, for his eyes glowed with exaltation, a smile of triumph played about his sensitive little mouth, and his whole being was suffused with a light of wonderful self-approbation.

At the head of the stair he turned and faced the assembled company once more, gazing at them as if from an immense height.

'I declare this meeting adjourned!' he cried with tremendous authority. 'As Acting Head of Department, I declare this meeting adjourned.'

VISITORS
Elizabeth Burns

The bell is chiming for early mass. This is what pulls her from a dream, though her eyes are still closed as she clambers out of bed and fumbles for clothes. Then the cold of the stone floor on her feet jolts her awake.

Sister Philippa puts on sandals, and runs across the shadowy courtyard, catching in the cool air a drift of scent from Sister Sophia's freesias on the windowsill. She slips into the back of the chapel where the rhythms of the mass are like a lullaby. She breathes the old smells of incense and candle smoke, and takes on her tongue the familiar melting of soft rice paper.

When the mass is over, the nuns, humming snatches of plainsong, wander out into the startling brightness of the light reflected off the convent's whitewashed walls. The little black-clad figure of the priest can be seen scuttling across the courtyard, and then on the donkey track as he makes his way back to the monastery.

The nuns drift into the dining room. It is low-ceilinged and dimly lit: at breakfast only thin shafts of daylight filter through the tiny east windows. In the gloom, the nuns munch caraway bread with honey and sip cups of warm goat's milk. Under the clatter of cutlery on crockery there is a murmur of voices.

After breakfast, Sister Philippa goes down to the garden to collect the eggs. The garden is set below the convent, sheltered from the winds off the Aegean by a wall. The sea winds can be harsh; for months Sister Philippa has had to wrap an old cardigan around her shoulders when she's come out to feed the chickens or fetch water from the spring. Her first winter at the convent, she could not sleep for the cold. But she looked on it as a suffering inflicted by God which had to be endured and lay awake for hours, shivering and repeating the rosary,

21

thinking it was her desire for worldly comfort that had to be broken, until Mother Lydia began to notice her nodding off during prayers, and asked if she were not sleeping. 'Everyone finds it bitter here, their first winter,' she had said, giving her more covers. 'Don't think you're being weak.'

In the henhouse Sister Philippa nudges the heavy squawking birds as she gropes for eggs. She's still frightened of the hens, whatever Sister Sophia may say about all God's creatures being worthy of our love, because of the way they snap and peck her fingers. Back in the garden she allows herself to stop for a moment and gaze at the sea as she breathes in mouthfuls of clear air, fresh-tasting after the stench of the henhouse.

Now that it's spring, the island feels as though it's waking from sleep: the opening of crinkly new leaves, wildflowers everywhere. Poppies, especially the poppies. Sometimes Sister Philippa has to kneel down by the side of the donkey-track and finger the frail silky petals, which, pressed between the pages of her missal, will turn a deep purplish red. Scattered over the hillside they look like drops of blood, 'A reminder for the Easter season,' Mother Lydia tells them every year, 'a symbol of the shed blood of the Saviour.' Almost Easter: they will begin blowing the eggs soon, and saving the hollow shells to decorate with indigo, saffron and madder dyes that colour the spaces on the eggshells left untouched by the wax of trailed candlegrease.

Sister Philippa carries the eggs she's collected, some with straw and downy feathers sticking to them, into the kitchen. A jug of lilac has been placed by the big enamel sink, and Sister Sophia, with smudges of flour on her papery cheeks, is kneading bread. Sister Philippa offers to help.

'But don't you have visitors to attend to?' asks Sister Sophia.

'They won't be here for a while yet.' Sister Philippa takes a piece of dough from the bowl and begins to pound it. Because she is the one who speaks the most English, and also a little French, the visitors are her responsibility.

'It's beginning to get busy, isn't it?' says Sister Sophia, sprinkling flour on the table. 'There's two ferries a day coming in from the mainland now.'

Sister Philippa nods. It's true: suddenly there are boatloads of people arriving on the island and some of them will follow the little maps in their guidebooks and climb up to visit the convent. But it makes her feel guilty, talking about the visitors, even though – or because – they are her greatest pleasure. They come for half the year like some kind of opium that she spends the other months waiting for. She punches at the dough as though it were herself.

It happens every year with the coming of the visitors, this falling away of faith. During the winter, sunk in the rituals of the convent, she does not question her vocation, but now, with travellers arriving every day from all over the world, a part of her wants to slip off and go with them when they leave the island. She's distracted from the life of the convent: day-dreaming of places like Ireland, India, Australia, she slops milk, drops plates on stone floors. And worse, this distracted-ness has seeped into her prayers as well.

Praying has become difficult. It used to be easy, as talking to her parents had been when she was with them every day, before the convent. Then she came to the island and now there are only letters, thin and stilted, and her mother cannot read or write, so it is left to her father to write down laboriously what his wife dictates to him: that the goat has had kids, that the oil is good this year, that her cousin is expecting another baby. Prayer is like that now: it feels paltry, and an effort.

Sister Philippa has never been in love, but she remembers how it was with her older sister: how she would come home late at night with her cheeks flushed and her eyes shining in the light of the candle, and the fragrance of orange blossom like a perfume on her, for she would have flowers of it in her hair. Then she would whisper of kisses, and of how he had carried her across the ford so she would not wet her feet. But nowadays her sister and her husband never speak to one another, except to bicker and nag. Sister Philippa supposes that to lose faith is like falling out of love. However much she wants to, she cannot go back to the days of ecstasy, of shimmering vision, to the innocence of the time when she took the veil.

Perhaps a different convent, she tells herself. But there

would still be walls. The walls are what, in nightmares, close in, and make her, waking, jealous of the footloose travellers, so that now with Sister Sophia she feels awkward and sinful and kneads her lumpy bread in silence. Sister Sophia has finished her loaves, and is covering them with cloths before she sets them to rise on the shelf below the window.

'I'll go out on the roof and look now,' says Sister Philippa, rubbing dough from her fingers. 'The visitors might be arriving.' And they are: she can make out two figures, a man and a woman, weaving their way up the hill. She leans over and looks down on the fragments of the village that she can make out: the harbour, the terracotta roofs of the houses and the walls bright with geraniums and nasturtiums. Those and the poppies: pink, orange, red, the colours splashing against the grey-white rock of the island, against the blue of the sea.

It's a long climb from the village to the convent. She's done it often, leading the donkey laden with fish or vegetables, sometimes with a piece of furniture or a bale of cloth. The visitors, both of them tall and blond, dressed in whites and pastels, come slowly up the hill: she watches them stopping at every turn of the path to look back at the view.

Now they've stopped to have a drink: the woman is bringing a bottle from her backpack. While they're resting, another woman catches up with them. Sister Philippa sees them offering her a drink, and then the newcomer takes out a map and spreads it on the ground and they all pore over it, then turn and look up the hill, pointing to the convent. The woman who has joined them is small and dark: her skin is an almond colour and her hair is black against a shirt that's the deep red colour of peonies.

After a while, Sister Philippa hears voices. She recognizes American accents, and looks down to see the three of them clambering up the wide steps cut by the monks out of the white rock. She waves, and points the visitors to the door of the convent. Standing there on the ramparts, she looks like a huge black bird. When she waves, the wide cloth of her sleeve flaps like a wing. The three faces look up, the golden-haired Americans grinning, and the dark woman sad-looking for a moment, before her face breaks into a smile and its lines disappear.

Sister Philippa is ready at the door in the wall when they all arrive some minutes later. She welcomes them to the convent on the hill. The Americans say 'Hi' as they shake her hand, and the other woman greets her in Greek, but with a strange lilting accent. '*Español*,' she explains. Her cheeks flush a dark red, the same colour as her shirt.

Now Sister Philippa must give them old clothes to cover themselves while they are in the convent. The young American man is wearing only shorts: she hands him a frayed shirt and an old sheet, indicating that he must wrap it around his waist. The two women both have bare shoulders, and the American one is bare-legged too. For them, Sister Philippa offers faded old print frocks that have lost their buttons. They wrap these garments round themselves, the Americans giggling a little, the Spanish woman silent, clutching the frock around her. Her arms next to its creamy cotton are very brown.

Sister Philippa leads them, awkward in their strange garments, out on to the roof from where they can drink in the view: the still, blue-green Aegean, the other islands faint and blurry, the village whose landmarks they can point out.

She always takes them there first, up to the roof, because it is her own favourite place in the convent. Water is visible, the edge of the island is visible, and the walls do not seem so very impenetrable. Their seclusion should be looked on as a gift, Mother Lydia tells them. 'God has placed you here for a reason. Accept it, don't fight against it,' she says. But sometimes Sister Philippa is frightened: it's as though all the nuns are rattling around in a box on top of a rocky hill on an island, and there's no escape.

After a few minutes she joins the visitors on the roof, speaking to them in her broken English and with gestures. The Spanish woman points down the hill, where two more figures have appeared on the path. They are a grey-haired couple, each with a walking stick, and dressed alike in trousers and plaid shirts. They are still far down the hill, too far away to notice Sister Philippa waving, and she does not like to shout:

she's embarrassed by the echoing of her voice against the rocks.

The sun is strong by now, and the wall has become almost too hot to rest bare flesh against. Sister Philippa beckons the visitors down and into the cool, stone-floored kitchen. She pours them cupfuls of spring water from the pitcher, giving it to them like a priest giving wine, and they sip it thirstily, dry from their climb. Then she offers them the host, the plate of sweetmeats, dusty with icing sugar that clings to their damp lips.

While the three of them are eating and drinking, a bell rings, and Sister Philippa hurries to the door to find the grey-haired hikers, arrived more quickly than she had expected. She apologizes for keeping them waiting, but the rosy-cheeked woman, in careful English, dismisses the apologies. 'It is wonderful to arrive!' she says, gesturing down the hill all the distance they have come, but she adds that they're from Switzerland, and are used to higher mountains than this. 'You speak very good English, better than me,' says Sister Philippa. The woman is pleased to be complimented. 'Every Monday evening I go to my English class,' she says. Her husband nods and smiles though he does not understand what is being said.

Sister Philippa takes them to the kitchen to meet the other visitors, and gives them sweets and water. After they too have glimpsed the view from the roof, Sister Philippa leads her flock out of the kitchen and along a corridor cluttered with chairs and pictures of the saints. Rosa-Maria often sits there, it's where she likes to be to watch who comes. The sisters mutter that she'll frighten away the visitors with her queer looks. But she smiles at each of them, her eyes behind her thick glasses glancing backwards and forwards along the corridor as the visitors squeeze past. As it is near Easter time, extra candles have been sent for, and Rosa-Maria has persuaded Mother Lydia to let her have one. She sits now in her huge chair, legs dangling in the air, rubbing the thick cream-coloured candle along her upper lip where she can feel its smoothness and smell the wax with its faint scent of honey.

At the end of the corridor, Sister Philippa opens the door with the key that hangs around her waist like a jailor's, and warns the visitors of the lowness of the lintel. The room is kept in darkness so that sunlight will not fade the colours of the embroidery or yellow the linen. Now, entering the room, Sister Philippa opens up the shutters and lets the light flood on to the folded piles of white cloths that lie on the big wooden table. In between them are little baskets of holy trinkets that glitter in the sunlight.

Sister Philippa feels embarrassed, showing off the wares. 'What about the traders in the temple?' she had once asked Mother Lydia. 'We have to make a living,' Mother Lydia had replied, 'and the visitors enjoy buying souvenirs.' But still she feels a little awkward, and stands in the corner between the heavy oak wall cabinets where the most precious work – the lacework and the finest woven shawls – is kept, together with the treasures of the convent: old pewter chalices, silver plates, dishes edged with intricate gold-leaf filigree.

The Swiss couple buy two pairs of slippers, for their grandchildren, it is explained. The Spanish woman chooses a small embroidered tablecloth. The Americans touch everything, unfolding cloths and exclaiming over them, but in the end buy nothing. Sister Philippa puts the money in her leather pouch, then opens a drawer underneath the table from which she brings out tissue paper and twine and wraps the purchases.

The visitors wander off down the corridor, while Sister Philippa locks the cabinets and closes the shutters. When she comes back out into the bright courtyard, she meets the Americans taking off their borrowed clothes. They hand them back to her and then the woman digs in the pocket of her shorts and brings out some coins which she presses into Sister Philippa's hand. 'For your work,' she says, with her wide white-toothed smile.

The Swiss couple clamber down from the roof where they've been photographing the view, and come and say goodbye. The four of them leave together, Sister Philippa watching from the door in the wall as they set off down the path. She'll go back to the rooftop and watch them as they wind their way down the hillside, disappearing among the pine forests, and then, tiny figures only recognizable by the colour of their clothes, reappearing on the path for a little before vanishing among the houses of the village.

She has begun, some days, to have imaginings of going with the visitors, of running after them along the piney path, down to the harbour and on to a waiting ferry. And then to the mainland, the city, Europe, America. Once she is on that boat she could go anywhere in the world. She could strap a rucksack on her back like these other women do, and be off, bare-legged, bare-armed, her hair growing dry and brittle in the sun.

Sometimes in dreams she is running down to the harbour where a rusty boat waits on placid turquoise water, where no waves break. The boat has been at anchor for hours, but as she is about to reach the harbour, the gangplank is pulled up and the boat sails away.

She cannot speak these thoughts to anyone. If they knew how restless the visitors made her feel, she would not, she supposes, be allowed to attend to them and her main pleasure in the summer of the convent would be lost. It is these thoughts which make her falter now in the courtyard, staying to stroke the flamy petals of the tulips instead of going back up to the roof to watch the disappearing visitors.

She looks up to see the Spanish woman coming out of the chapel. She's blinking in the strong sunlight, and tears are falling down her cheeks. She brushes them away with her hand when she sees the nun, who goes to her and lightly touches her arm. The Spanish woman looks down and shakes her head. When she looks up, she's trying to smile, but more tears fall. 'My sister,' she says, slowly. 'She is dead.'

'A candle?' Sister Philippa asks, pointing to the chapel. The Spanish woman nods, and then shrugs as if she doubts it will do any good. Sister Philippa takes her hand, which is strangely cold. 'Tea?'

The Spanish woman says softly, '*Evharisto*,' thank you.

Sister Philippa takes her into the cool of the kitchen, and finds some of Sister Sophia's herbs that she uses for tea. She boils up the dry leaves to make a pale green-gold liquid.

'Renata,' says the woman, pointing to herself.

'Philippa.'

They smile. Renata buries her face in the jug of lilac. 'Good,' she says, breathing in the scent again. When the tea is ready, Sister Philippa pours it from the little tin saucepan, and they carry the cups out to the garden and sit under the lemon tree where tiny green fruits are beginning to appear. Against the stone wall the purple-blue irises rise as stately as candles.

At first Sister Philippa had avoided the convent garden: it seemed too much like being in her father's smallholding, and she preferred the indoor tasks at the convent. But going out there with Sister Sophia, who knew the name of every flower and herb, she began to enjoy the smell of earth and garlic flowers on her fingers, the feel of the soil as she patted it around a new plant.

They sip the pale tea. Renata's hands run over the grass as though they were ruffling hair. She picks up a few flowers of lemon blossom and places them in the lap of the faded frock. 'My sister –' she says, suddenly, not looking up from the blossoms. But then it seems there are no words, and she simply touches her heart and clasps her hands together tightly. 'She is dead,' she says again, and the lines on her face are like creases in cloth that cannot be ironed out. Then she points to herself and makes a gesture of emptiness, shrugging her shoulders. 'I go to France, Italy, Greece – Turkey? Africa?' She shakes her head, at first gently, and then more violently.

Sister Philippa does not know the English words she needs for comfort. There is nothing to do but to hold Renata's hunched shoulders under the worn cotton of the frock, and then to let her sob and sob with her face buried in the black cloth of her habit, leaving it damp with tears.

The bell for lunch begins to chime. They stand up and wander over to the door in the wall. Sister Philippa half opens the door, and then stands fingering the blisters in the paint-work that is hot to the touch in the midday sun.

Renata takes off the frock. Her shoulders are very smooth and brown, like the henhouse eggs. She reaches with her bare arm to push the door open wider, and points out of it across the path to the olive grove a little further up the hill. Then she mimes eating, and opens her little rucksack to show that she has food.

'Yes?' she asks. 'Yes?'

Sister Philippa thinks of the long tables and the sunless room, of other elbows always at her sides. She remembers picnics, how they used to be when she was a child. She is slowly folding the old frock into a little bundle, then she lays it down beside the tub of geraniums at the door. She should tell someone she won't be at lunch. But she shrugs her shoulders in a gesture as though she herself had taken off the extra garment and felt lighter, and the two women go out, closing the door behind them. Sister Philippa has not noticed the face of Rosa-Maria, peering out through the arched window in the corridor, nor her hand, waving goodbye.

They cross the track and walk past the old barn where the vines cling, and up the slope of the olive grove, so that they are looking down on the convent, and, far away, the sea. They sit beneath the trees, on ground scattered with crisp fallen leaves, and olive stones pecked bare by the birds. Renata takes food from her bag: bread, goat's cheese, oranges. From her pocket she brings a penknife. Then suddenly she smiles, and fumbles again in her bag. She brings out the tissue paper parcel Sister Philippa has wrapped for her, and cuts the twine with her knife. Then she lays out the cloth on the bumpy, dusty ground, and sets the food on it. It seems strange to Sister Philippa to see one of the novices' white cloths with its blue and crimson cross-stitch set on the ground, where, as they eat, insects, and once a tiny lizard, crawl across it.

After the bread and cheese, Renata carefully peels both oranges, and hands one of them to Sister Philippa. When she has eaten her fruit, and licked the sticky juice from her fingers, Renata leans back against an olive tree and takes off her sandals. Her long toes wriggle in the grass, and she smiles and closes her eyes as the sun dapples her face.

Sister Philippa feels hot and enclosed in her black. Always black, as though she constantly mourned. 'We do mourn,' Mother Lydia would say. 'We are in mourning for the death of our Saviour and for the sorrows of the world.' But what about the resurrection, Sister Philippa wants to ask her, why not light and colour?

How would it feel to have the sun on her bare skin? This too happened so long ago that she has forgotten the sensation. While Renata's eyes are closed, Sister Philippa rolls up the sleeve of her habit to the elbow, and examines the whitish flesh, then leans back on that arm so that it is out of the shadow and in the sun. It feels as though a liquid as warm and gold as honey is dripping on to her skin, and even though the palm of her hand begins to hurt from the rough ground it presses on, she does not lift it.

They sit like that for a long time. When she opens her eyes, Renata points to the sea. 'Tomorrow,' she says.

'Where?' asks Sister Philippa. Renata takes out her creased map and traces her route with her finger: another of the islands, then back to the mainland, then – she raises her eyebrows in a question – and swirls her finger around the map of Europe eastwards.

Sister Philippa looks over to the islands, and sees figures coming up the hill. She tells Renata she must get back for them. They stand up and brush the twigs from their clothes. Renata picks up the orange peel, shakes the crumbs from the tablecloth and refolds it, then wraps it loosely in the tissue paper.

'Goodbye,' she says, taking Sister Philippa's hands in hers, and kissing her on each cheek.

Sister Philippa stands watching as Renata sets off down the track, turning back twice to wave before she disappears from sight into the pine forest. And here are the other visitors already, almost at the convent. Sister Philippa runs down through the olive grove, and is ready, breathless, at the door to greet them.

PASS THE PARCEL
*Gordon Burnside**

'. . . AT CATTERICK, THEY'RE INTO THE FINAL FURLONG
AND IT'S HOLY GRAIL BY HALF A LENGTH FROM GET
THE MESSAGE WITH HURRY BACK A LENGTH AWAY THIRD
AND TIRING, THE OTHERS ARE OUT OF IT . . .'

Someone swore and walked out of the shop.

'. . . IT'S HOLY GRAIL AND GET THE MESSAGE, NOTHING
BETWEEN THEM . . .'

In the centre of the room, head bowed, eyes closed, Sandy,
a huge lump of a man, clutched a pink betting slip to his chest.

'. . . HOLY GRAIL, GET THE MESSAGE, GET THE MESSAGE,
HOLY GRAIL, THEY'VE GONE PAST TOGETHER, WE'LL
WAIT FOR IT . . .'

Sandy trudged to a corner of the room. He leaned his forehead
against a *Sporting Life* pinned to the wall, and began praying:
'Get the message get the message get the message . . .'

'. . . PHOTO FINISH CATTERICK . . .'

Doreen ambled to the far end of her catwalk. Just above
the back of one knee, watched by Davie, licking his lips through

---

*AUTHOR'S NOTE ON PRONUNCIATION
The phonetic spelling in 'Pass the Parcel' represents the Dundee dialect.
   Of particular importance is the Dundee 'e' sound, pronounced as the
'e' in wet. 'E' follows this rule and means either 'I' or 'yes', depending
upon its context. 'Meh peh', meaning 'my pie', would have the same
'e' pronunciation.
   Glottal stops are compulsory, but assumed.

toothless gums, a penny-sized bubble of flesh wobbled through a hole in her black stockings.

'. . . HORSES IN THE PHOTO . . . NUMBER TWELVE, GET THE MESSAGE . . .'

Doreen slashed a red mark to the left of the number twelve on the list of runners.

'. . . AND NUMBER ONE, HOLY GRAIL . . .'

She stretched to reach the number one and her skirt hitched up, showing an inch or so of pale flesh puffing over the tops of her stockings. Davie took off his bonnet, and fanned himself with it. Doreen straightened her skirt and tucked in her blouse, tugging it tight.
'They top-weights'll be the daith o' me!' said Davie.
'Yi don't say,' said Norrie.

'. . . LOOK OUT BRISTOL . . .'

'E'm lookin', E'm lookin!' said Davie, and wheezed into a laugh.
'Yi're easy amused, E'll say that fur yi,' said Norrie.

'. . . RESULT CATTERICK . . .'

Sandy turned from the wall. 'Get the message, get the message, get the message . . .'

'. . . FIRST NUMBER ONE, SECOND NUMBER TWELVE . . . FIRST NUMBER ONE, HOLY GRAIL . . .'

'Bugger-bugger-bugger-shite!' said Sandy. He crumpled the betting slip and threw it against the wall.
Doreen turned and pointed at him. 'Sandy Wilkie! E'll no tell yi again!'
Sandy looked at the floor.
Norrie waddled over to him. 'Did yi win, Sandy? Did yi loss?'

Sandy tutted and rolled his eyes upwards. Norrie put a hand on each of Sandy's shoulders, and looked up at him.

'Yi didni loss did yi? How much did yi loss? What is it? It's a mug's gemme. What is it?'

'A mug's gemme.'

'Yi never sayed a truer word. How much? Come on, how much did yi loss?'

Sandy pulled at his bottom lip.

'A thousand pound. But dinni tell mi sister!'

Norrie covered his face with his hands.

'Sandy Sandy Sandy. What're wi goanni dae wee you Sandy Wilkie?'

'Dinni tell mi sister, eh no?'

'Shi'll no hear it fae me. A thousand pound! How much is that this week?'

'Fev million!'

Norrie whistled, and shook his head.

'Did yi hear that, Doreen? Sandy's drapped anither grand. That's fev million this week.'

A few customers laughed.

'That's right,' said Doreen, 'hae a good laugh. How wid youse feel if yi lost ae million, never mind fev.' She gave Sandy an annoyed look. 'But that's no the point. What aboot oor night oot the night? What aboot oor date? E suppose that's it aff, is it?'

Sandy blushed, grinning madly.

'E'll tak yi oot Doreen,' said Davie.

Doreen folded her arms and looked at Sandy. 'E'm waitin,' she said. Sandy looked at the floor.

'Lave the lad alane,' said Norrie. 'It'd tak a better ane than you ti capchir this fella. You tell ir Sandy. What's a man gotta do? Tell ir.'

Sandy shuffled towards Doreen. He stopped and looked back to Norrie. Norrie nodded.

'A man's gotta do what a man's gotta do,' said Sandy.

Doreen smiled. 'You're a heart-breaker Sandy Wilkie. C'mon, time ti meet yir sister. Did yi mind a'hin?'

'Twa boneless kippers . . . twenty Craven A . . . six number fev eggs an dinni drap thim . . . twa Askit pooders.'

34

'Good,' said Doreen. She picked up a Tesco carrier bag from behind the knee-high partition and held it out to Sandy. 'Awa yi go now. See yi the moarn.'

Sandy took the bag. 'Cheerio then Doreen.'

'Cheerio.'

'Cheerio then Norrie.'

'Cheerio Sandy.'

'Cheerio then Davie.'

'E, right.'

Sandy left.

'E'll tak yi oot Doreen,' said Davie.

*

When the betting shop closed for the day, Norrie met Doreen outside. It was Norrie's giro day, so they were going for a pub tea in the town.

'Sport. Who did Ian Botham play football for? Scunthorpe United, Tranmere Rovers, Plymouth Argyle?'

'Scunthorpe,' said Norrie quietly and forked the last of his lasagne into his mouth.

The two men playing the Trivia Quiz machine agreed that the answer was 'Tranmere' and one of them pressed the button marked 'B'. The machine made a rasping sound.

The other man smacked his forehead with the heel of one hand. 'Plymouth! He played for Somerset!'

Norrie got up from the table and took hold of the empty glasses.

'Entertainment. Which Shakespeare play features two pairs of identical twins?'

'Not a clue,' said one of the men. He covered his eyes with one hand and stabbed blindly with the other, hitting the button marked 'C'. The machine beeped a tune.

'Yes!' said the man, punching the air and laughing.

'Quick! History,' said the other. 'Where is Waterloo? France, Spain, Belgium?'

'Follie the smell,' said Norrie, and made for the bar.

When he came back with the drinks, the men had stopped playing the machine.

35

'It was Scunthorpe,' he said as he passed them. They looked at him blankly. 'Botham. Ee played fur Scunthorpe. It wuzni Plymouth it wuz Scunthorpe.' The men turned away.

Norrie clunked the drinks on to the table and sat down beside Doreen.

'Smert-erse!' said Doreen. She topped up her glass from the tin of Diet Coke.

'E've half a mind ti dae somethin' aboot it,' said Norrie.

Doreen glanced at the men.

'Act yir age,' she whispered. 'Yi asked fur it. Naebody likes a smert-erse.'

'What're yi on aboot smert-erse What's smert-erse aboot askin fur a joab?'

Doreen laughed.

'What's funny? I'm no laughin.'

'Naither am E. E thought . . .' She nodded towards the two men. 'E thought yi wir aggravated at they twa.'

Norrie looked over at the men, then said loudly, straight at them: 'They twa! E widni wipe mi erse wee they twa!'

The men carried on talking for a moment, then put their unfinished drinks on top of the machine, picked up their briefcases, and left. Doreen watched them go, then turned and glared at Norrie. Norrie lowered his eyes. Doreen picked up her drink and gulped it down. She thumped the empty glass on to the table and grabbed her coat. Norrie sighed and tapped ash into the ashtray.

Doreen pulled her coat on, but one arm went inside a tear in the lining. She tried to pull it out, but her charm bracelet stuck. She gave it a tug and the lining began to tear.

Norrie looked up, and stifled a smile. Doreen glowered at him. She wrenched her arm free bringing the lining, bracelet still attached, with it. Norrie snorted. Doreen closed her eyes, bared her teeth, growled, then hung her head.

'C'mere,' said Norrie. He got up from the table and began to disentangle the bracelet.

'E'm sorry,' he said. 'Yi're right. E wuz out of order. E wuz . . . There yi are, that's you now.'

Doreen tucked the torn lining back into the arm hole.

'E've sayed E'm sorry,' said Norrie. 'C'mon Doreen, dinni

tak the huff. Doreen c'mon. Look, sit doon fur a meenit till E feenish mi drink, eh? Then wi'll git up the road. What di yi say?'

Doreen tossed her coat over the back of a chair. She picked up her glass and the empty tin of Diet Coke and held them out to Norrie.

Norrie pulled a face, then took them and headed for the bar.

Norrie poked at the stubs in the ashtray with the tip of his cigarette.

'Thir must be some'hin wi kin dae,' he said. 'What aboot the Trades Descriptions Act, kin wi no git im on that?'

Doreen shook her head. 'Waater under the bridge.'

'But the advert sayed male or female. Ee shouldni git awa wee it. What aboot "Equal opportunities"?'

'Forget it,' said Doreen. 'Yi canni bate his kind. Yi sayed it yirsell. Thir wuz only you an him on the phone. It's your word against his. Jist forget it, eh?'

Norrie snapped his fingers and pointed at Doreen.

'The Sex Discrimination Act! E'll go up and see im an ask fur an interview in front i witnesses.'

'What gade'll that dae?'

'E'll tell yi what gade it'll dae. If ee turns iz doon in front i witnesses, E'll git im under the Sex Discrimination Act!'

'Look, the man's no stupid. Ee'll jist tell yi the joab's tane. Dinni wyste yir time. Even if ee diz gie yi an interview, ee dizni haeti gie yi the joab, diz ee?'

'Ee shouldni git awa wee it!'

'Ee shouldni, but ee diz, an thir's nothin' yi kin dae aboot it. Now, c'mon, drink up an wi'll git up the road an E'll show yi meh sex discrimination act.'

As they passed the Trivia Quiz machine, Norrie punched the button marked 'C'.

'Scunthorpe!' he hissed.

*

Sandy was standing at his usual spot outside the library, clutching the carrier bag to his chest, mindful of the eggs. A bus passed up Victoria Road, and he thought he saw someone waving from a window on the top deck. He would have waved back, but he had the eggs to think of.

He walked over to a low wall, and sat down. Carefully, he took the messages out of the carrier bag and lined them up on the wall. 'Twa boneless kippers . . . twenty Craven A . . . six number fev eggs . . .' He opened the box, then closed it again.

'Hiya Sandy!'

Sandy looked up.

'Hiya Norrie. Hiya Doreen.'

Doreen smiled.

'Hiya. Checkin yir messages, eh?'

'E.'

'Yir sister awa gittin a book?'

'Is shi?'

'Is shi? Yir sister. Is shi in the lebbry?'

'Shi musti missed ir bus. Shi sometimes misses ir bus. E wish shi'd hurry up, E'm caald.'

'Are yi shair it's here yi're meetin' ir. Is it no someplace else?'

'Ootside the lebbry!'

Doreen looked at her watch, then at Norrie. Norrie pointed at the messages on the wall.

'Shi canni be lang now. E'd git they back in yir bag afore thi faa aff the dyke, if E wuz you. See yi later, eh?'

'E, see yi later,' said Sandy.

Norrie and Doreen looked out at Sandy through the smoked glass doors of the library.

'What di yi think?' said Norrie.

Doreen took a cigarette from her packet and rummaged in her bag for her lighter.

'Well, shi's no missed ir bus. It's nearly seeven. Shi musti hid an accident or some'hin.'

'What'll wi dae?' said Norrie. 'Phone the police?' He nodded to a sign on the wall. 'It's no smokin.'

Doreen lit her cigarette. She inhaled deeply, and hissed the smoke out through her teeth.

'Shi might turn up yit.'

'Act yir age,' said Norrie. 'Ee left the bookie's at half past fower. That's twa an a half oors ago. It's a joab fur the boabbies.'

He nodded to Doreen to look behind her. A uniformed attendant looked from her to the 'No Smoking' sign and back again.

Doreen took a long drag on her cigarette. She pushed the door open, and exhaled into the open air. The attendant looked away and walked off.

'Gie some folk a uniform!' said Doreen. She took another drag on her cigarette, then flicked it out of the door.

'Na,' she said. 'The police'd jist fleg im. Wi'll tak im hame wirsell.'

Norrie sighed.

'How kin wi? Wi dinni ken whar ee bides. Ee mair then likely dizni ken eezsell. An what if eez sister diz turn up? What if shi's waitin someplace else? What if shi's already tellt the police? An apert fae aa that, what maks yi think ee'd come wee us? If yi waant meh opinion, E think wi should keep oor nose ooti it an let the boabbies git on wee it.'

'Oh, that's what you think is it?' said Doreen. 'If E mind right, you were aa fur bidin on the bus . . . Look at im.'

Sandy was sitting on the wall, the carrier bag clutched to his chest.

'Look, E'll tell yi what. Wi'll ask im whar ee bides. If ee kens, wi'll tak im hame. If ee dizni, yi kin phone yir boabbies. OK?'

Norrie sighed.

'OK.'

Sandy knew his address.

'S. Wilkee – one oh three – Fintry Gardens – North Dundee!' he chanted.

'Fintry Gairdens,' said Doreen. 'That's no far fae us. Yi kin chum us up the road on the bus.'

'Fintry Gairdens!' said Norrie. Doreen glared at him.

Sandy chewed his bottom lip.

'Meh sister sayed ti wait fur hur an no ti go wee strangers.'

39

'But we're no strangers,' said Doreen. 'Are wi?'

Sandy shuffled his feet and looked at the ground.

'No. But E always wait fur ir. Shi's missed ir bus afore.'

'Fintry Gairdens,' said Norrie. 'That's in Fintry is it no?'

'Brilliant!' said Doreen. 'Fintry Gairdens is in Fintry. What di yi think i that, Sandy? Will wi gie im a medal?'

'No, look,' said Norrie. He took a newspaper from his back pocket and opened it out. 'E wuz readin it on the bus. Look at the haidline.'

He turned the paper towards Sandy, and gave Doreen a warning look. The headline read, 'New Factory for Dundee?'

'Fintry . . . Bus . . . Drivers . . . Strike,' said Norrie, pointing to each word of the headline in turn. He handed the paper to Sandy. 'That's how yir sister's no here, Sandy. She couldni git a bus. Thi're on strike. Look.'

Sandy gaped at the paper.

Doreen looked at Norrie, who shrugged. She smiled a tight smile, and shook her head from side to side.

'C'mon then Sandy,' she said. 'Wi'd better git yi up that road afore yir sister sends oot a search perty.'

Sandy handed the paper back to Norrie.

'That's yir workin man fur yi,' said Norrie. 'Nae consideration. What di yi say Sandy?'

'A man's gotta do what a man's gotta do,' said Sandy.

Since the buses 'weren't running', they had to take a taxi.

Sandy was worried that his sister would be angry. Shi'd be needin ir fags an pooders an the kippers wir fur thir tea an ee wuzni supposed ti go wee strangers an Doreen an Norrie wereni strangers but mibbee eez sister wid think thi wir cuz ee kent thim fae the bookie's an eez sister didni ken ee went ti the bookie's cuz ee wuzni supposed ti an mibbee the eggs had went foostie cuz it wuz late an eez sister aye pit thim strecht in the fridge. The fridge was a goad-send cuz in the aald days eggs wuz aye goin' foostie an sometimes yi got a wee daid chicken in thim.

Doreen put his mind at rest. The tea wuzni a problem. The eggs'd keep. So wid the kippers. Sandy an hur'd git drapped aff at the chipper. Norrie'd tell eez sister thir wuz a fish supper

40

on the waye. Ee'd say they worked in Tesco's and kent Sandy fae there an saw aboot the buses in the paper. Thir wuz nothin ti worry aboot. Naebody wid mention the bookie's. A'hin'd be hunky-dory.

Doreen and Sandy got out at the chip shop and the taxi dropped Norrie off at Sandy's tenement.

Sandy had said he lived on the ground floor. There were two doors facing each other. One had no nameplate, so Norrie checked the other one. The nameplate on that one was broken but the last three letters of the name were still there.

Norrie rang the doorbell . . . No answer. He tried again . . . Nothing. He knocked, rang the bell *and* knocked, but there was no answer.

He pushed the letter box open and peered in. The lobby was in darkness and all the doors off it seemed closed, but he could hear the TV. He tried shouting through the letter box and knocking at the same time, but no one answered.

Norrie swore. Ee should've asked Sandy fur the key. Mibbee ane i the neebirs hid ane.

He tried the other door . . . No answer. He went upstairs and knocked on one of the doors . . . A man's voice shouted 'Fuck off!' He tried the other door . . . A dog barked and gouged at the inside of the door, but no one came.

On the top floor, a middle-aged woman said that she'd just moved in an didni ken anybody in the close, but shi wuz shair the ither hoose on that landin wuz emmpy cuz shi'd hid the pick i the twa hooses an anywaye yi kid see the boarded-up windeez fae the road.

Norrie went back downstairs. He rang the doorbell again, knocked, and shouted through the letter box. He could still hear the TV, but no one came.

Mibbee Sandy's sister was oot lookin fur im . . . But the TV wuz on . . . Mibbee shi wuz sleepin . . . But that racket would've wakened the daid . . . Mibbee shi wuz daif . . . But shi wouldni sit waatching TV wee ir brither waanderin the streets. An shi wuz supposed to be meetin im . . . Mibbee shi wuz oot lookin fur im . . . but the TV wuz on. Mibbee shi'd hid an accident . . . but the TV wuz on. Mibbee shi wuz no weel . . . Or daid.

He took a cigarette out of his packet, remembered he didn't have a light, and put it back. Treh the windee!

The thin net screens made it difficult to see in. Norrie cupped his hands over his eyes. He could only make out vague shapes, lit by the flickering beam from the TV.

He knocked on the window . . . nothing. Mibbee ee could get in through a windee . . . Locked. Treh the windees roond the back . . . He ran through the close. Locked. Mibbee the door wuz open! He ran back into the close . . . Locked.

Norrie sat down on the bottom of the stairs. He took his cigarette packet out of his anorak pocket, then put it back. If Sandy didni hae a key, it wuz definitely a joab fur the boabbies.

Sandy marched into the close, followed by Norrie and Doreen.

'E looked through the letter box,' said Norrie. 'Thir's nae key there. E'd i saw it if thir wuz.'

Sandy put the carrier bag down carefully. He opened the letter box with one hand, put the other one in and pulled out a Yale key on the end of a string.

Norrie pointed to the other door, the one with the broken nameplate.

'Wha bides there?'

'Aald Mrs Reekie,' said Sandy, putting the key into the lock.

Norrie sighed, and scratched his head.

'Here, E'll dae that Sandy,' said Doreen. She handed him the parcel from the chip shop.

'Norrie'll go in furst an tell yir sister what's happened, then shi'll no be angry at yi.'

She opened the door and turned to Norrie.

'Wid it no be better fur you ti tell ir?' said Norrie. 'You bein' a wummin, ken. Me an Sandy'll wait oot here.'

He picked up the carrier bag and gave it to Sandy, taking the parcel. Doreen glared at him, then went into the house, pulling the door almost closed.

'The chips'll git caald,' said Sandy.

'It'll no be lang now,' said Norrie. 'Awa you an waatch oot the closie in case yir sister's oot lookin' fur yi.'

42

Norrie pushed open the door in time to see Doreen disappear into a room at the far end of the lobby. A few moments later, she came out again. She closed the door behind her and, head bowed, walked slowly towards the front door.

Norrie whispered her name. She looked up, sighed and shook her head from side to side, then, putting a finger over her lips, gestured to him to come in. Norrie checked that Sandy was still keeping lookout, and stepped into the lobby.

'Shi's no is shi?' he whispered.

'Stane caald.'

Doreen took two cigarettes from her packet. She lit them both, and gave one to Norrie.

'Yi kin phone yir boabbies now.'

Norrie nodded in the direction of the front door.

'What aboot . . . ?'

Doreen rubbed her forehead with the tips of her fingers.

'Lave him ti me. Say yi're awa fur fags an tell im ti come in.'

Norrie turned to go, then turned back and handed Doreen the parcel. He turned again to go, then stopped.

'What'll E say if ee asks?'

Doreen inhaled deeply and hissed, 'Jist git, will yi?'

Doreen met Sandy at the door.

'Yir sister's sleepin,' she said. 'Wi'll hae wir tea in the kitchen no ti waacken ir.'

Followed by Doreen, Sandy tiptoed down the lobby into the kitchen. He took the messages out of the carrier bag and put them on to the kitchen table. He opened the fridge and put the kippers on a shelf. One by one, he took the eggs out of their box, eased them into their hollows in the fridge door, then closed it carefully, making sure it was properly shut. He folded up the carrier bag, laid it on top of the fridge, and arranged the empty egg box, Askit powders and the packet of cigarettes on top of it.

Doreen opened the parcel from the chip shop and put one of the fish suppers on to the table.

'C'mon now, sit doon an eat yir tea afore it goes caald. Jist yase yir fingers.'

She lit the grill on the cooker, turned it to low, and put the

43

parcel in the grill tray, on top of the grill. She sighed, turned off the grill and sat down at the table, opposite Sandy.

'Sandy,' she said, 'mind E sayed yir sister wuz sleepin?'

Sandy spat a mouthful of fish into one hand.

'Stane caald!' he said.

*

Doreen squatted at the end of her walkway, sipping a cup of tea. Apart from Norrie and Davie, there were only three other customers in the betting shop.

'Perts i the boadee?' said Davie.

'Perts i the boadee,' said Norrie. 'Simple as that. Echt teams wee perts i the boadee in their name.'

He took two cigarettes out of his packet, and tossed one to Doreen. Davie scratched his nose. Doreen lit her cigarette and threw her lighter to Norrie. Davie flipped his bottom lip with a finger.

'Perts i the boadee . . .'

Norrie lit his cigarette and went over to Doreen.

'Arsenal!' said Davie.

'Trust you!' said Norrie. 'That laves seeven ti git.'

Davie hurried over to the far side of the room. He took a football coupon out of a dispenser fixed to the wall.

'That's chaitin,' said Norrie.

'What's fur tea,' said Doreen. 'An dinni say fish. E'm seek i fish.'

'Fish,' said Norrie.

Davie zig-zagged a finger down the coupon . . .

'Liverpool!'

'Six ti git.'

'Manchester! Baith i thim.'

'Fev ti git.'

'Man United an Man City. That's twa!'

'Twa teams, one pert,' said Norrie. 'Fev ti git.'

He flicked the lighter on and off, and handed it to Doreen.

'It's aa go,' he said.

Doreen yawned and stretched her arms high above her head, then tucked her blouse back into her skirt, tugging it tight.

'Bournemouth!' said Davie.
'Very good,' said Norrie. 'That laves fower an afore yi ask, Bristol dizni coont.'
'Herts!'
'Three ti git.'

'. . . LATEST BETTING HACKNEY. AT HACKNEY THEY BET . . .'

Doreen dragged herself upright. 'Goin' ti the doags,' she groaned.
'Di yi gie in?' said Norrie.
Davie took off his bonnet and clawed at his scalp, then tossed the coupon away.
'Right!' said Norrie.
He clapped his hands and rubbed them together. He touched the tip of the pinkie of his left hand with the index finger of his right.
'West Ham!'
'What?'
Norrie smirked.
'Yir ham's yir theh!'
Davie tutted and rolled his eyes upwards. Norrie moved his index finger from the pinkie to the ring finger.
'Brechin.'
'Brechin?' said Davie. 'Brechin!'
Norrie smiled a clown's smile, and pointed to his chin.
'Bree-chin!'
'Fuck's sake!' said Davie.
'Hiya Doreen! Hiya Norrie! Hiya Davie!'
Sandy was standing, half in, half out of the door. Norrie moved towards him.
'Well dinni jist stand there yi daft bugger! C'mon in.'
'E'm no supposed ti,' said Sandy.
Norrie grabbed Sandy's hand and pulled him in along with another man who was holding his other hand. The man was wearing a duffel coat with the hood up and as he was pulled in, he put his chin tight to his chest and turned away.
'Well well well,' said Doreen, clambering down from her

45

walkway. 'You're a sight fur sare ez, Sandy Wilkie. Wha's yir pal?'

Sandy grinned.

'This is Roderick. He's meh pal. Ee's affy sheh.'

Norrie moved round beside the other man and bent down, trying to look at his face. He took the man's free hand and gave it a waggle.

'Pleased ti meet yi Roderick.'

Roderick tried to bury his chin deeper into his chest.

'Lave the lad alane,' said Doreen. 'That's a bra coat yi've got Sandy. Yi're a right smasher. Aa the lassies'll be efter yi.'

'E,' said Sandy.

'Sandy! Roderick!'

A well-dressed woman in her twenties came hurrying into the betting shop, out of breath.

'There you are! You shouldn't be in places like this. C'mon now. Out!'

Norrie moved towards her.

'It's meh fault, darlin. Sorry. It wuz me that haaled im in.'

The woman looked Norrie and Doreen up and down, then hustled Sandy and his pal out of the betting shop. Norrie was about to follow her, but Doreen stopped him.

'Did yi see the waye shi looked at us?' said Norrie.

'Shi wuz jist faird,' said Doreen. 'Shi'd be worried aboot ir joab. Forget it, eh?'

She took two cigarettes from her packet, lit them both, and gave one to Norrie.

'Ee's lookin bra though,' she said.

Davie picked up the football coupon from the floor.

'The ither boy wuz ane i they mongols,' he said. 'Turn yir stomach. What was the last ane?'

Norrie glared at him.

'What did you say?'

Davie looked up from the coupon.

'What wuz the last ane? The name i the team?'

Norrie looked at Doreen. She smiled a tight smile, and shook her head from side to side. Norrie took the coupon from Davie. He crumpled it into a ball and threw it away.

'Scunthorpe!'

46

THE WALL
Mercedes Clarasó

The soldiers came and demolished the village. It took them only a few minutes. They drove a tank through the single row of huts that constituted the one and only street. The huts crumbled like matchboxes, and by the time the tank had reached the end of the row there was nothing left but a dense cloud of dust hanging over a long heap of rubble. The soldiers drove on, laughing, to demolish the next village.

After the silence had been complete for some time the people began to creep back cautiously from the forest where they had hidden as soon as the scout arrived with the news that the soldiers were on their way. By now the dust had settled and the villagers were able to see the line of rubble that had been their homes. One of the middle huts had somehow managed to retain one standing wall – the front one, with its door and tiny window – almost as if nothing had happened. The only difference was that the rectangles of door and window, instead of showing up dark against the white wall, were now bright with the early morning sunlight streaming through them, making the wall look darker in comparison. This reversal of the natural order made it clear at once that the rest of Leocadia's hut had not been spared. The façade stood there like a parody of a triumphal arch, as the ironic centrepiece of the long line of ruins.

As the people came out of the forest and saw what had become of their village they began to wail. First one voice, then another, rose in a loud and piercing lament. The people advanced, and the wailing grew in volume and intricacy, into a weird and complex fugue of desolation and despair. Each family was drawn to their own little plot of rubble to lament over their private loss. Gradually, still wailing, they gathered in front of the one standing wall. Leocadia stood among them, silent, facing her own open door. It was as if they all expected some sort of sign or command from this one remaining symbol of their community. Gradually the wailing began to die down, then stopped abruptly. The unrehearsed ceremony of lamentation was over, and the people dispersed. Now each went to his own plot to see what could be rescued. Leocadia was left standing alone, still silent.

Soon, scraps of conversation could be heard from the various groups, and families began drifting away, carrying as much as they could in the way of food and belongings. No farewells were said: it was taken for granted that they were all heading for the same place – over the hills, to the more peaceful regions in the hinterland.

'Leocadia, you are alone, you must come with us. We must all help each other.'

'No, Maria, I stay here.' Leocadia looked at her next-door neighbour of more than forty years and reflected that this might be the last time they ever saw each other.

'But Leo, it's not safe here. They will come back. And if they don't, others will. You have no one to protect you. Not even a house to live in.'

'I have a wall. I still have my front door. That's more than you have.' Leocadia smiled gently.

'And what use is a door, in God's name? And what use is a wall without a house? It won't even keep the rain off you.'

'It never rains. You know it never rains now.'

'Well, it won't even keep the sun off you.'

'Yes, it will. All morning its shade will keep me cool here, in the street, and all afternoon I can take shelter on the other side, where my house used to be. Only at midday . . .'

'At midday you will be roasted like a peanut in a burning fiery furnace.'

'Only for a few hours. We can all stand a few hours of discomfort.'

Maria's husband now appeared. 'You're coming with us, Leocadia. You can't travel alone.'

'No, Pedro, I must wait for my son.'

'He may not come, Leocadia.'

She bowed her head in acknowledgement.

48

'He has been gone many months.'

Again she bowed her head. 'But I must wait.'

Pedro and Maria exchanged glances, unconvinced. Then Maria tried again.

'But you cannot stay here without a house. And the soldiers may come again.'

'They would kill you,' put in Pedro.

Leocadia smiled deprecatingly. 'I am very old,' she said.

'But you are strong and active, you can easily keep up with the rest of us.'

Leocadia smiled again, almost apologetically. 'It's not that. How can I explain? When you are young you say, "I must have this thing to be happy, I must have this other thing to be safe." But when you are old – truly, blessedly old like me – then things don't matter so much. This thing or that thing, you take from them what you wish. So I shall wait here. If my son comes, that is good. And if the soldiers come, that is good too.'

'And if no one comes?'

'Perhaps that would be best of all.'

By now all the other families had gone. Maria and Pedro bade a ceremonious farewell to their neighbour and set off, carrying as much as they could. After they had advanced a few yards Maria turned and called back, 'Leo, you will find half a sack of meal in the corner by the window. We've taken all we can carry. Have it, with our blessing.'

Leocadia bowed her head and spread out her hands in a gesture of acceptance. She watched her friends till they had disappeared over the crest of the hill, then she turned round to face the front of her house, and stood there, very still.

She was doing penance. I shouldn't have left the village, she thought, I shouldn't have left it unprotected. When the news of the advance of the soldiers had come she had decided to stay. She didn't know how a solitary old woman could withstand the soldiers and their tanks. But she had a strong conviction that this was what she ought to do. As the oldest member of the community she would intercede for the village. Perhaps they would listen to her. Who knows, perhaps one of them had met her son, and for his sake would spare the village.

But she had let herself be flustered and frightened by the fear of the others, scooped up by their panic in the uneasy half-light of dawn.

Now she stood in front of the devastation that through her own weakness she had not managed to prevent, trying to recover her centre. She had lost what might be her last chance of doing anything for another human being. She had bungled it. Now she had to recover her harmony with the physical world, with this little part of the earth's surface that she knew and belonged to.

After a while of emptiness she began to lay her plans, to settle how she was to live this next, and perhaps last, phase of her life.

She would do as she had said to Maria, get as much shade as she could from her one remaining wall. She wandered about among the ruins till she found a little rush-bottomed chair a few houses away. Anselmo's chair, she thought. He will not need it. He will not grudge me it. She thought of how often she had sat on it outside Anselmo's front door, and dusted it carefully with her apron. Then she carried it back to her own house. At that precise moment she had no need for it, as the sun was so high that neither side of the wall afforded much shadow. However, she set to, and, having cleared a space near the door, she placed the chair in it, so that it would be ready for her when the sun once again agreed to share its power with the shadows. Then she moved to the corner of the hut where her bed had been – still was, in fact, though buried under a large portion of roof. Carefully and without hurrying she cleared the debris off the bed, took the bedding out through the front door and, obeying an urge to keep to the familiar rituals, shook it out thoroughly. After that she brought it back in again and carefully remade the bed on top of the debris she had cleared off it. If I can't sleep under my own roof, she thought with a smile, at least I shall sleep on top of it.

Next, she hunted about till she found a few utensils to eat with – a tin plate, a spoon, a cup. She decided not to bother making a fire. She would eat the meal soaked in water, that would do well enough. The prospect of living at this very basic level filled her with a certain satisfaction. It was a new beginning, with all the excitement and stimulation that this brings, and at the same time a return to a more primitive stage. It wasn't that she didn't appreciate the good things of this earth – she had thoroughly enjoyed the few and simple luxuries that had come her way. But she had always tried to limit her needs and her desires, not through asceticism or a desire to punish herself, but out of an unshakeable conviction that there lay contentment. The more you have, the more you want, had been her motto.

Having found a mound of rubble near the door, where her table used to stand, she placed a flat piece of wood on it. Now she had a table again. Before putting her small assortment of implements on it she reflected that it would be better with a cloth. Finding one of the curtains relatively undamaged she gave it a good shake and installed it as her tablecloth. Now all she needed was to see to the water and the corn supplies, and she would be ready to start her new regime.

The well, which was a few yards beyond one of the end houses, was undamaged. Even the bucket and rope were in perfect order. She drew water and carried it slowly to the new version of her home. Now that there was no one else in the village she could just leave the bucket there, inside her front door – or outside, in the morning, she decided, to take advantage of the only source of shade. She could have transferred Maria's half sack of corn to her own house, but delicacy forbade her to do this. It belonged to Maria and Pedro, and in their house it must stay, even if they were never to come back, even though they had given it to her. But she would gladly help herself to a portion, morning and evening, always remembering to give thanks in her heart to the givers.

After her meal, sitting in the shade behind her wall, she looked out of her doorway on to the familiar sandy surface of the road. Apart from a few pieces of debris left lying about, all she saw looked perfectly normal. An ant hill near her door had been trampled on, and the ants were busily repairing the damage. They're doing just what I've been doing, she thought, only better. But then, they had a purpose to fulfil together. Her purpose was now a solitary one. She sat for a long time watching the ants with great concentration, reflecting that never before in her life, not since early childhood at any rate, had she had at her disposal unlimited time to sit and do nothing. It was pleasant, she thought, a good way of growing. Life had cast her in the role of one of the Marthas of this world; but the Mary inside her, developing slowly and fitfully, could now come into her own. She had always been a doer and a helper and a contriver, coping with gusto in the face of poverty and difficulties. Now for the first time there was nothing to do. No one needed her help – not the help of her hands, anyway.

For days she sat there, reliving the incidents of her life one after another. How, she wondered, could people talk of being lonely, with this unending procession going on inside? All her friends were there, her children, her husband, neighbours, strangers, all the people she had ever known, the living and the dead. Even people she had merely heard about, they were all there, familiar from the words of her companions. Now that there were no things to be done, no people to interrupt her, she held discourse with a refreshing company. Many, if not most of them, were dead, but that made no difference.

Over the years she had noticed that she grieved less over each succeeding death as it took place. It was as if the boundary between life and death became more blurred as the years rolled on. She thought of the bitter grieving of her youth over the death of her first child. She recalled the loss she had felt when her husband had died all those years ago; and now it all seemed a mistake, an unnecessary agony. And she thought of her one remaining son, long overdue from his journey. But she thought of him without fear, even without apprehension. The wall that separated the living from the dead was becoming increasingly fragile. Her son might be on this side of it, he might be on the other. Either way, it didn't much matter. It was all a question of time.

This blurring of the frontiers between the living and the dead was an affective thing. It was not in any sense a case of mental confusion. She knew very well who was living and who was dead. It was just that she felt as close to the one as to the other. She had come to feel that death was a relatively unimportant stage in the development of all living creatures.

Every night she slept very peacefully in her bed under the stars, almost without dreams. When she got up she always stood for a while outside her door, facing east, as she had done that first day when the huts were knocked down. But now she stood calmly, without the self-reproach of that first day. She had failed then but now her failure was over, now she had another part to play in this arid strip of world that was still her home. She was trying to become perfectly, totally at one with this wonderful patch of dusty soil. She wanted to belong to it as completely as the ants moving lightly over its surface. She wanted to become the place itself, just as the dry and dusty road was the place and the dark green forest beyond was also the place. She wanted to assume the consciousness of this piece of soil that she had known and served all her life.

On the seventh morning she woke up more refreshed than ever. She was sure she had had no dreams, just a long consciousness of sleep and rest. And with it an awareness that someone was travelling through the forest, coming towards her. She got up and stood as usual in front of her wall, facing east, with her back to the forest. She had no idea how near or how far the traveller was, and felt no temptation to turn and look. Her seven solitary days had washed away all curiosity or impatience. She imagined the swish of the machete clearing a path through the forest. She stood there waiting for the actual sound to come to her. Perhaps the traveller was her son. Or perhaps a stranger. Or perhaps the hand that wielded the blade was carrying not a machete, but a scythe.

TSANTSA
Erik Coutts

As worlds went, this one was a lie.

This he'd always known. But now even the shamans were on the run and all the while they went into the reaches and left their truths to wander the woods like spells.

He wanted a beer. Even called for one. But his voice went hoarsely round the thatch and then there was just the sound of the night losing its power. Who'd make his beer now? Or crop the plantains that no man's hand should touch? And who should entice the Nungui so she'd make the roots go deep in the night? Or lay the three pieces of jasper by the roots that she might rejoice in Motherhood? Where should *he* lie in the close dark?

Truly this world was a lie. This he'd always known. But now such lies even seeped into the real world, seeping like disease. Perhaps dreams had lost their truthfulness?

And he went through the flags of dark and stepped over his wives' dead limbs and lit the copal torch and put it into the thatch and there was a tree of flame. Then he took the curassow from its perch and whispered to it and stroked its neck feathers that it might not be afraid, and when it settled so he could see the fires widening in its eyes, he wrung its neck and laid it on the floor.

When his house had burnt out, the dawn was coming over the line of the high leaves. Of the house, only its blackened ends remained and they stood up like the ends of a swamped boat. And when he squatted and thought awhiles he found his foot had crusted in his younger wife's menstrual blood, for he'd quit the house through the women's door. He made to remove the dark crystals. But again he set to thinking, and went in silence and bitterness to the gable and kicked it down with his heel and the ash ran to meet him. There's your family,

he told himself. Then he took the muzzle loader, and the
blowgun, and he threaded the darts into his hair and went to
the point where the Yaquipa sounds like doused flame.

He corded himself to the trunk of a palm, and he knew he
was scared. When he'd drunk maikura there had always been
someone to hold him down, maybe stop him running just
anywhere. So he made a thick knot about the cord and he
drank down the maikura faster than he ever had, and he
placed the darts away from him and he bunched his thighs
until they hurt. He started to shake. Someway off, he heard
his legs banging on the root trails. There was an anvil on his
heart. And when the lightning of his vision came, he hung on
to the tree, for there, about him, was the arutam, the first
vision – and a new one, and it scared him more than any in
his manhood. The arutam took the form of two anacondas,
and they came at him in the same entwined thickness. The
trees were breaking in the lightning, and smoking where they
split, and roaring, and he was sore with fear. But he let out a
yell that it might see him through, and he leaned forward and
touched the heads of the snakes – and there was an explosion
and, before him . . . the true arutam, the final vision.

The old man, the same. And straightaway, he said, 'I am
your ancestor, and just as I have lived a long time, so will you
live a long time. And just as I have killed many times, so will
you kill many times.'

When he faded, the dawn was mingling into his shape, and
the witness felt the power – the soul – was such as he'd never
known; he was shaking with the need to kill. His teeth were
chattering, but his smile drew them quiet, and he lay back on
his tired bones for he knew another dawn should break before
he roused.

When the full power of the arutam-soul was stable within him,
he found he could walk steadily and he went into the reaches;
went as far as the head waters of the Yaquipa; carried the
muzzle loader and the blowgun, the darts again threaded into
his hair. And though there was an elation about his heart, he
again recalled how this world was a lie – saw the ash of his
children, studied the dark life of his wife's blood.

55

He'd hunted these reaches many times, even with his older wife, for she'd leashed the dog and come on behind – they'd taken an ocelot which he'd traded for cutting tools. But always, he'd carried a lesser power within his blood, a thing of small consequence, easily confessed. And this he recognized clearly enough, unafraid now, obligated by his manhood and his years.

On the stills, his kinsmen were taking fish; he helped; he ate the crab they gave him. These cousins too were troubled by the seepage of lies – yet they would house him only the one night, wouldn't go with him in the morning. They sensed the power of his arutam, and this scared them; the days of a man were finished, they told him, the world now balanced only on a lie.

'Why worry?' his cousin said, in the mestizo style, 'I can take just the one hide in the high summer, and for that they'll give me enough to visit my son in the stockade.' (His cousin was no coward, but so he now spoke.) 'And that way I'll keep my nose clean and hold by the law. The days of taking the tsantsa are finished and I'm through talking of this.'

Once, he'd come to this house of his cousins and the feast had been like no other. He brought his brother with him so none might shoot him in the back when the feasting ended, and he'd drunk more beer that night than any in the three districts. In those days, there were tsantsa feasts in every household and much power was received, even by the women. But that was over and even his family were gone and their power was nothing.

But he settled down with his cousins on stools and drank beer through the depths of the night and at dawn they put out their torches on the old times. His cousin's wife gave him manioc so he should not hunger on the trail. And he went out, and over the small outcrop of the Cordilleras that strains any but a man in the fullness of new power: he came on the lumber camp from the escarpment that he might be shaded as he watched.

It had long been debated whether the whites possessed arutam-soul and mainly it was felt they lacked such power. They conferred only lies and measles. But now, as he watched them with the mestizo kids, he wondered whether this too was a lie. It seemed to him the whites possessed something as strong – maybe stronger – but vile in its power, like the spirits that wander the woods when evil quits a corpse. Hadn't he seen a man – renowned in killings as himself – shot down in his tracks just as his power was at its highest? Shot by these same whites who brought measles? Who took the world and broke it into charcoal that rode over a man's ankles?

All lies!

Maybe their power was the lie that waited to be born? That which should drive men into the finest ash? With its birth, their end? The stronger the man, the finer his ash.

Such were his thoughts as he watched the big gasps of smoke, the haze, the settled blue. There were many whites here; a few in white coats like the kilts of women. And these lived in two tents with all the authority of chiefs and delivered their measles into the arms of the kids so they might infest the woods, strike at men and their families, break them. Even the shamans, even they should break.

He blew on the edge of the leaf. And when the toucan came to the sound, he sent a dart through its neck and took the brighter plumage to the house of his son-in-law. The man was on a hunt, so he spoke with the younger wife – his daughter – and when he told her of her mother's death, he noticed the pieces of pottery clay at the corners of her mouth and only then realized she had the strange needs of pregnancy. When his daughter asked how such a power could take them all so quickly, her sisters also, he told her of the poisonous power of the whites. Then the son-in-law returned, and he carried just the one squirrel monkey, its arms like stone.

So they butchered the monkey, and settled, and sat on stools by the men's door, and the son-in-law learned how pervasive were lies. Then they drank beer and watched the women drawing the clusters of peanut from the garden. The younger man pondered lies; watched the shimmer of the high leaves. Then he agreed to this one raid, maybe the last ever about the head waters of the Yaquipa, maybe the last in this whole lying world. But he asked too, for a day's leave that he might bring in more game, for they were sick of crayfish and the women moaned incessantly, even the younger wife despite her craving for clay.

So they went into the forest and the older man took the tube and blew tobacco smoke into his son-in-law, and he swallowed the smoke better than he'd ever done. And this pleased them and they smiled and then waited like statues until they brought down a squirrel monkey. But the son-in-law confessed his heart wasn't in hunting: the tsantsa worried him more than he'd let on. So they went back and drank beer and talked of lies and the falling-in of the world.

'Surely I am strong with the need for killing,' the older man said, 'but when I have confessed my arutam and the power starts to ebb, I'll take nothing more from either the true or the false world.'

'But the tsantsa will be the truest taken by men,' the other said, and he was pleased that he now provided reassurance for the older man.

But as quickly, he too fell to gloom and spoke no more until they had cleared the hard ribbons of the Cordilleras. And they went through a second dawn and lay by the vale where the whites slept.

And the two men crouched by the gully, knelt in the mist hanging there. And, as decreed, each in turn confessed his arutam, the younger man's now feeble, almost spent, the other's so fierce it began to ebb in pain even as he spoke. He knew well that when a man loses all his soul in this fashion, there is no power in a tsantsa, and he clung to the bank in desperation and pressed his lips on the dirt as if, there alone, truth might open up to him.

There were two tents, and the three whites plus the three whites made six whites, and likely armed with Winchesters, so the men went furtively round the trash cans and their weight of needles. And these were finer than monkey bone, yet as long, and they made for a sombreness in the pair of them, and they touched nothing.

They waited, the cord of the tent running between each man's view of the other's eyes, each smiling secretly, sometimes fretting in thought. The older man could feel the blaze taking him about the heart, and when the sound of the first white stirred in the tent, the blaze was an agony. Now – he thought – even as the power ebbs this fast. And he took the machete and went at once and struck down the white as he came into the clean air, and the white went forward on three drunken steps and down the red loam and stopped on the bottom of the gully. About this man, there was still the slow flourish of night – the stale dark – and this was good for it made the best kind of tsantsa, and when they'd finished, they went in their rolling way up the far bank and through the sunlight.

Here there was cover, and big forest beyond, laid in smoke, but the mestizos had brought a horse trail from the station below the Cordilleras and now this carried heavy traffic from the sawing plant, so the men went around this trail and felt fierce surges in their blood. They rested-up. Then they worked rapidly. In their pouches were charcoal, needles, black bees-wax and combs, and about their kilts there were lengths of bark twine.

Three times they stopped on the trail. This the tsantsa decreed, for its power ebbed like a man's soul would ebb, so they captured its power by stages, found time to heat the pebbles at a fire and roll them within the tsantsa. And later they washed and groomed its spiky hair and drew the twine across the fine white teeth and put the toucan plumage into braids and hung them at the ears. It took them three days to come winding back, preparing, taking the tsantsa's new power as they came – and when they reached the son-in-law's house, there was a cordon of washed night settling in the leaves.

And so they discovered the sickness. The younger wife lay in the far shadow, and the child also, and both were groaning and lathering. And the older wife came through the dark and her feet were heavy, and she told them she was fevering also, and in her belly was an agony and it rose even as she spoke. Then she went over and lay on the man's bed – for she no longer cared – and she put her arms high above her into the dark.

The older man sat on a stool. He wanted beer, but said

nothing. Truly, it was all a lie! And its power was beyond a man.

The last crusts of his wife's blood were still between his toes. He tried to see her face. Then he threw the tsantsa against the far wall, and there was a dark ribbon of plumage, and when it stopped rolling, it lied to him through its swollen lips.

RUNNING AWAY
Robert Dodds

I'm sure I'm not the only man in the world whose wife has
run away. But generally the lady actually absents herself by
car, or train, or simply by omitting to return from the super-
market. Now my wife really *did* run away, moving off at a
steady pace, while I poured myself coffee from a thermos
jug. I watched her through the windscreen of our parked car,
speckled with insect deaths, and from his car seat our three-
year-old son watched too, his mouth stuffed with currant cake.
We didn't grasp the situation at all, Thomas and I, as her
figure dwindled into the distance.

We were on our way to Rosemary's parents. A longish trek
which we often punctuated with a picnic stop somewhere on
the uplands of Wiltshire. This was about our half-way mark.
It can't have been Thomas that upset her. He had been no
trouble. True, he had thrown up outside Stevenage. But then
he had given us fair warning, and the bulk of the affair was
conducted with decorum on the hard shoulder. Nor had Rosemary herself seemed troubled at all – no hint that such an
extraordinary thing was going to happen.

It was a Thursday. In August. Warmish, a few fluffy clouds
blowing across a mainly blue sky. The car was packed with
the usual paraphernalia – all Thomas's junk and of course my
golf clubs and fishing tackle. I didn't like to be kicking my
heels too much around Rosemary's parents' place. Lovely
place of course – big house, lawns, shrubberies and so on. But
every time I urged our Skoda past the heraldic whatnots on
the gateposts I began to feel intimations of inferiority. Drawn
by the sound of tyres on gravel, the old biddy generally
stations herself at the head of the steps to the front door.
Daughter and grandson receive their welcoming simpers. I
drag behind, snail-like, with the suitcases, and her look

suggests that although the trail of slime I have left on the steps is invisible to others, she can see it well enough. And I've never felt very at ease with the colonel either – not since the day I made the mistake of talking politics. Hence the golf and fishing gear.

I suppose that in many respects I was very lucky to marry a girl like Rosemary. She was – is – a few years younger than me. Tall, lively, attractive. I'm pretty quiet myself and somewhere around the middle of the spectrum when it comes to looks and height. But inches aren't everything, and sometimes I remind Rosemary (and she agrees) that she's better off with me than hitched up to some horsey county type and bored to death in a swamp of gin and tonic. As a school-master's wife in a small town she's got a valuable social function. Or she had.

People have been very kind. But I made a mistake telling the truth. No one believes a word of it, although they all pretend to. They think she's gone off with another man, or back to mother. The usual things. They won't accept that she just vanished. I don't suppose I would unless . . . well, I'm getting sidetracked. I was describing to you the events of that Thursday in August. The day it happened.

Bit of a tiff as we set off. This was normal. I had insisted that Thomas eat up every last bit of his muesli before we left. Rosemary was of the opinion that if he didn't feel like it, he should leave it. Events near Stevenage proved her right, on this occasion. But in general she over-indulged him.

Once in the car, we listened to Radio Three most of the morning. Rosemary prefers pop music, but she can listen to that all day in the kitchen, so when we're in the car my taste prevails, by common assent. Thomas likes any sort of noise, so he's happy. I remember it was some rather 'difficult' twentieth-century stuff – Schoenberg I think – and Rosemary commented on how music in a car always made her feel like she was in a film. The Schoenberg apparently made her feel she was in a film about nuclear holocaust, looking out at the last moments of a dying world.

The spot where we left the main road for our picnic was an old favourite. A small lane rose between sparse hedges up and over a hill, away from the sound of the traffic. Then you were into another world. The round backs of the downs rolling away as if without end. Fields, mostly grass, but some with yellow wheat or barley, dotted with poppies. We turned off the lane on to the beginning of a widish straight path, a chalky line rising gently upwards across the down and disappearing against the sky. I switched off the engine and we wound down the windows. We didn't speak – even Thomas didn't speak. We just listened for a moment: the wind rustling in the barley stalks and hissing in the grass, insects humming, a skylark, the sounds of cooling metal and settling liquid from the car engine. The peace of it. The calm of it. I shut my eyes for a few moments.

Rosemary packs a good picnic lunch. We had some excellent sandwiches: avocado and cream cheese with a hint of Marmite in granary bread. We didn't talk much. I rack my brains to think of anything in particular we might have said. Thomas was feeling better. I told him the names of some of the things we could see – a barn in the flatter fields away below the downs, some cows grazing there, the difference between cumulus clouds and alto-cirrus. Rosemary thought just 'clouds' would do for a three year old. It was the word she'd used all her life. However, I didn't take up swords on that one. I felt very calm, contented, happy almost – as you sometimes are in simple moments of peacefulness, looking at the world, thinking of nothing in particular.

We'd nearly finished eating when a little flurry of breeze took a paper napkin out of the car on Rosemary's side. Her window was open, and it whisked out as if with a mind of its own, and set off up the path, tumbling and flapping along.

I know Rosemary's inclination would have been to let it go. But I have a horror of litter, of which she was well aware. We watched it for a minute or so as the wind took it along the track. Although it wavered and wandered a little, it nevertheless had the air of a rambler, setting off on a favourite walk, and making good progress. It must have been fifty yards away when Rosemary said, 'I suppose I'd better go and grab it.' I hadn't said anything mind, and I just picked up the thermos and started to unscrew the top, for a refill of coffee.

Rosemary got out of the car and set off after the napkin. Thomas wanted some cake, so I twisted around and gave him a piece, which he dropped. By the time I'd sorted him out and turned around again, things seemed to be taking a rather comical turn. The wind must have picked up a bit, and the napkin was further away than ever, a hundred yards maybe, and bowling along. Rosemary had started to run. She was wearing jeans, and a white blouse. Blue and white on a green, blue and white backdrop. As she got further away, the napkin well ahead of her, the scene seemed to have a humorous futility about it.

Thomas chuckled a little through his cake. 'Mummy's running away from us,' he said. I explained that Mummy was *not* running away from us, but after a piece of litter. Then he said, '*Why's* she running away from us?' so I left it and said, 'I don't know.'

The napkin was now a tiny white dot, still, amazingly, proceeding along the path. Equally amazing was Rosemary's persistence. She was fully two hundred yards away now, apparently running hard. The wind was gusting strongly, and the barley in the field beside the car rattled furiously in a wave-like riffling motion. It sounded like laughter.

It was when Rosemary had dwindled to a distant silhouette against the brow of the down that a horrible sort of feeling washed over me. A physical feeling in the pit of my stomach, and a prickling of the hairs on my neck and the backs of my hands. A flock of crows appeared from nowhere and flapped noisily overhead. They distracted my attention for a moment, and when I turned back to look for Rosemary, she had gone.

I spoke to Thomas, to reassure myself. 'Mummy must have gone bonkers Thomas!' He laughed. 'Bonkers. What's bonkers Daddy?'

'It's running off into the blue horizon after a scrap of paper,' I replied.

We waited. I sipped my coffee thoughtfully. It calmed me. Rosemary would reappear at any moment, at the brow of the hill. I tooted the horn a couple of times. She would come back down the long white path, clutching the napkin in triumph, glowing with exertion.

How long would *you* wait in such a situation? Five minutes passed. I was angry. Thomas kept asking where Mummy had gone. I turned on the radio but it was just crackle. I kept on looking at my watch, setting a limit after which, surely, she *had* to reappear. Thomas started to cry.

After ten minutes I'd had it. I was furious, but I was also worried. A mixture of odd thoughts came into my head: had Rosemary fallen and broken her ankle? Had some extraordinary brainstorm? Been attacked by some lurking rural maniac? Where had that flock of crows come from so suddenly? How was it that the napkin never stopped or blew off the path? I calmed Thomas down as best I could and thought over what I should do. Thomas couldn't be left in the car alone, especially as he was already in a bit of a state. The path was too narrow to drive the car up. The only thing was to get Thomas out and set off together after Rosemary, hand in hand up the path.

Thomas was unimpressed by the prospect of going to look for Mummy. In the end I had to carry him, and I was pretty fed up and hot by the time we'd struggled up to where Rosemary had vanished. I'd been expecting this to be one of those false horizons that anyone who has ever climbed a hill is familiar with. But, to my surprise, we really were at a high windy viewpoint, right on the spine of the down, and the path fell away below us into a long valley. Well over a mile away, the ground began to rise again in a new series of hills, until the prospect was lost in a bluish haze.

In spite of my anxiety, I felt a strange exhilaration, as if I were an eagle soaring high above the world. I scrutinized the landscape for any hint of Rosemary's figure, but nothing moved except the clouds and the grass. Putting Thomas down to give my arms a rest, my attention was caught by something close at hand. A few feet ahead on the path lay the napkin. It was absolutely still, the wind not moving it at all. I walked forward to pick it up, but when my hand was inches away – whoosh! – the wind caught it hard and it flew twenty yards down the path, where it settled once more. I raced down towards it. Again it set off, tumbling away down the hill. I *had* to get hold of it. Somehow, once I had got it in my hands,

Rosemary would turn up again. Just then, a cry of 'Daddy!' brought me up short. I looked back. Thomas stood on the brow of the hill, looking down towards me, on the verge of tears. Already he seemed a long way off. With an effort of will I relinquished my chase, and climbed back up the slope to Thomas. I was shaking, my legs as unsteady as if I had run a marathon.

I sat down for a minute or two, and while I chattered about nothing to Thomas I continued to look intently at the landscape for any hint of Rosemary. I ignored the napkin, which didn't move. It had frightened me, the way it had seemed to pull me after it. In the end there seemed no point in going further on foot. I could see the path plainly for at least a mile ahead, and the surrounding fields were bare. It was as if she had flown up into the sky, transformed into a skylark.

I called out a few times, without much hope. Thomas was getting cold. I suppose we stayed up there for about a quarter of an hour, before turning back and descending towards our car, parked like a dinky toy down below. Nonsensically I expected to see Rosemary sitting inside when we got back, but she wasn't. Just her handbag and a half-eaten biscuit on the dashboard. I looked at the shape her teeth had bitten out. It was like a relic of a bygone age – a crusader's helmet or a fossil.

That, really, is the end of the story. I drove to the nearest village, where I found the local constable eating his lunch in the pub. He listened to what I had to say, and was very reassuring – he would get one or two people together and we'd all go out on to the downs that afternoon. If she was anywhere out there we'd find her all right. But of course we didn't. Nor did anything turn up in the following days, or weeks, or months. It has been nearly a year now. I go down to Wiltshire every other weekend, and I've come to know the hills in all their moods. White and silent under a sprinkling of snow; muffled and damp in shifting grey mists; dazzling green, blue and white, as they were on the day I lost her.

SCUM OF THE EARTH
Allan Mitchell Fowlie

I mean, what kind of bastard gives you your tin, your tobacco and your papers, then says he's keeping the matches for your own good. I've been rolling anyhow. I got a machine, but I can hand roll. I've made a full tinful – have them stacked, twenty, lying like a pack of ready-mades. Soon as they comes – I know they're coming back, I read papers, I knows about the bastards, they'll be coming back – and I'm going to have a light. I'm just going to ask them, tell them, 'Give me a light!' Then I'll just chain smoke – if it's keeping going. It's the only trouble with rollies.

They're taking my watch. How'm I supposed to tell how long I been here?

Just leaves you sitting. Nothing to do. Don't give a toss. I'm seeing stack of magazines, piled up – out there, shelf along the back. Nothing passes me – but they never thinks to offer. Stuff them. It's hardly mattering anyhow, there's hardly any light. Bet they're making sure of that – one poxy bulb, probably picks it for lack of watts.

Can't look out the windows even. It's one of them modern places – built like a lavatory – no bloody windows, except up by the ceiling, a strip along the wall. I stood on the bed, still couldn't see – need to be ten foot.

Bet they're turning off the heating. It's bloody freezing in here. Bastards. It's sort of thing they do. Leaves you one poxy blanket. I'm not using it – don't know where it's been.

They should be bringing us a cup of tea. I'm entitled. They always brings a cup of tea. I seen it on the TV.

I mean, what kind of bastard says he'll get a cup of tea, so you're waiting on it, then pisses off for bloody hours. If they'd bring the bloody cup of tea, I'd have a bloody light.

Could do with a video, something in here. Pass the time. Take your mind off – they wouldn't think of that.

Trouble is, I likes a fag and a cup of tea with a video. Or a carryout. And maybe's a take-away – Indian or something. Should make your own entertainment, my dad used to say – not watch tele all the time.

Tried having a wank – to pass the time – it's healthy. Makes you think of something else.

It's right that – it's what they're saying – it's healthy. I'm reading it. Annie Raeburn, or whatever, one of them, in the back pages in the woman's magazines – it's pretty good, they got all the stuff like you gets in a Jackie Collins, better probably – and it's saying, it's okay for blokes to be doing it anytime. Relieves tensions and that. I got tensions to relieve. Probably – medical fact this – stops you having heart attacks if you're doing it regular. It's exercise.

Not that I does it that often.

When I'm doing it – myself – I likes to think of bums mostly. Women's bums – I'm not going for blokes. Big bare ones – often thinks of stacks of them, groups of them, crowding in. They has to be big though. Maggie, who I lives with, she's common law, you know. She's got this great, really big bum. Nice, you know. I still likes it even now. It's part-way what's attracting us. Because I hardly notice tits. I mean, you know, obviously I miss them when they got none. But big or small, it don't bother me.

I'm not getting nowhere. You haven't the surroundings. It's not the sort of place – feels all embarrassed – keeps thinking I'm hearing them, sneaking up for a peep.

No one's coming. They're probably up the bar, getting pissed and geed up. I don't bloody care – can bloody stay there. It's preferable when I thinks about it. Don't bloody want them here – don't want them coming here. Can stuff their bloody cups of tea.

I don't want them turning up with tea. They'll be making sure it's boiling – burning us – throwing it in my face. If they've got matches, they'll burn us for definite. I know. They're bastards.

Could do with a pint though – myself.

Just nip out, be back in twenty minutes, piss off and have a pint. Wouldn't go to the local. Take the train right out, go right out in the country. Then I'd have a quick pint and when it's dark I'd hide. Stacks of places in the country, woods and hills and trees – maybes come across a cave. Even with a helicopter they couldn't find me. I'd be like that bloke, in the Hitchcock film, ducking and diving, going through streams, with cops coming down hills and still I'm getting round behind. I'm staying out a few days and hiding in my cave and maybe's I'm hearing them, because they're standing right by. They don't see me. I'm lying looking out, camouflaged all over. I just sees the legs and the big black boots. I could reach out, touch them, they're standing that close. They're having a breather, bit of a chat – saying how they're admiring us, because of how I'm dodging them. Then I hears on their radios, orders coming over, telling them to pack it in.

Even then, though I knows they're going, I stays another night. It's not so bad, because I'm taking the time, making it all comfy. Then when I wakes up, it's pretty late on and I'm waiting on the lunch time and I'm going back down, back in the pub. I'm having a pint, big piece of pie, bit of salad and that – maybes beans, a few chips, don't know, all depends. I'm just sitting at the bar, chatting away with the landlord there, because there's not many in – it's like he says, it's always the way, come middle of the week. He's telling us then, the way they do, by way of conversation, telling us, how he's always on the look out for experienced blokes. I has to say I'm interested, because I've done a bit of barwork. But I'm telling him straight off, I needs to be full time – which is suiting him anyhow – I'm looking for lodgings, it has to be live in.

It's how it's happening: we gets on really well, so I'm staying on ages and everyone round here, they're just left wondering.

Probably, it's hard to tell, but probably it's where I'd be now – be in the pub normally. A few pints, game of pool in the bar round the back. I likes a game of pool. I'm not one of them has to play all the time. Some of them, they spends a fortune. But I likes a game though – just now and then.

Probably they're all there – probably not playing – just mouthing off – calling us.

Bet I'm dead bloody topical. Not that it bothers me. I just takes it in my stride. It's not like they're mates. Prats mostly. Just blokes to have a pint with – maybes game of pool.

They all hates us anyhow. I can tell – I sees through them. Never wants to play with us. It's on account of how I'm beating them. Not every time exactly, mostly though. I mean, sometimes I goes in early and I'm putting down fifty 'p' on the table and I'm getting on and I'm still on come ten o'clock – last bell even. It's pissing them off. Some of them I beats dead easy. Like I'll be potting black and they're hardly starting, getting the brush nearly. On occasion, just for a laugh, I lets them get ahead a bit. Then I waits and when they thinks – you can see it on their faces, dead give away really – they thinks they're going to win, I gets on the table and I'm potting left and right, cleaning up. That's pissing them off especially.

Bet they plays snooker here, not poxy pool for them. Bet they're all crowding in, playing snooker upstairs. They always got a snooker room. It's how – I knows this for a fact, being told by a bloke who knows – it's how Ray Reardon's doing it. It's right that. Never bloody nicks no one, just plays snooker all the time. Bit of a shirker really. Probably if you asks them – other cops, who knew him then – that's what they be saying.

*

Bet they're bringing their cues when coming down here. Be pissed as arseholes – all fired up.

I knows they're coming down, be crowding in, filling the place and taking turns – kicking my head in, beating my bloody brains out. I knows it – I know. You hears things. I knows blokes.

Really – and I'm going to tell them and all – really I needs a brief here, barrister probably, sitting with us full time, not just for five minutes, doing all round the clock. Two of them probably, working shifts, so when they're having a piss. I needs protection – I'm bloody endangered.

Bloody cops. Pushing us, shoving us. All bloody crowding round, trying to take a look. Big bastard cop, sergeant or something, he's taking my name and writing it all down and this other cop's standing there, holding my arm, twisting it a bit really. I'm telling him – leave off. But the big bastard sergeant, he's just looking up then saying to us – dead nasty, 'Shut it!' Then he's telling me he wants my watch and empty all my pockets. I puts all my stuff down, spread out all over the desk. It's just crumpled up paper mostly, all different coloured tissues, used snot rags I carries. It's on account of how I'm having this bit of a bad cold – head cold, you know, I was laid up a few days, I'm not hardly over it. Bastard big sergeant, he's looking at the tissues, giving out like he's all disgusted and telling us to take them back, pushing them back at us, poking them with his pen. It's a bit of a flash pen really, Parker or something – bit flash for a copper – not that he's letting us use it when I comes to sign my name. He's just bunging us a cheap one he's taking from the drawer. But I'm getting a laugh after. When he's finishing his writing, I sees him, he's putting the flash pen up in his mouth – sucking on it, you know.

Then they're taking us off then, going down this corridor. There's stacks of them still, coppers all crowded round, just standing there, blocking the way, not letting us pass – not letting us pass and banging into us. Mostly it's blokes, but there's woman cops and all. They're just as bloody bad –

worse even – because – it's understandable really – you expects more.

Mate of mine – I plays pool with – he's got this great name for them. He's calling them – whispering it, if they comes in the pub – 'It's WCs full of pee.' I'm nearly saying it. I mean, I been acting dead casual, making my way through like it's not bothering us, and I'm thinking, maybes I should cut them dead then with the witty remark. I don't though – I just lets it pass, has a sort of an inward laugh.

Bunch of bastards – think they'd realize – I has rights – statutory and all. It's incompetence I calls it. Never taking note of circumstances – how it's happening, how I'm only trying to help.

It's right that. It's how it's starting. I'm only trying to help to start off. Give him benefit of what I learnt. Only doing like they says you should – on the tele all the time – take bit of an interest, check out his education.

It's him who's starting it anyhow. It's him telling us. Telling us how his teacher's saying he's backward with his reading. It's because he's watching too much tele, all them videos and that. So I says to him, explaining, fatherly like, the way you do – about how reading's dead important – should be doing it all the time. But he don't take a telling. He's just giving us a bit of lip. He saying, if it's so bleeding important how come he's never seeing us doing any reading. I doesn't let it get to us. I'm staying dead calm – like icy calm. I just gets up, gets down this book I got – been meaning to read – Jackie Collins a mate's letting us have and saying how it's dead good. I opens up the first page and I reads it out loud. I'm doing it spot on – near on for word perfect. Then I gives it him, tells him – do the same you.

He's not hardly even looking at it before he's saying how it's too hard. I has to clip him then and he starts taking the piss, starts crying straight off – like he's always doing, even though I'm not hardly touching him. I mean, what's he think I'm reading it for? I'm checking so I knows. None of it's getting too complicated – out of his capabilities – because you know – I mean, I realizes he's not hardly nine.

Even then, I has to give him a clip just to get him started. And still he's not hardly trying – hardly getting past the first few. Truth is, I has to say, he's starting to piss me off then. So I'm telling him, so he'll concentrate, sort of by way of encouragement – telling him everytime he's doing a wrong one, he's getting another clip. Not that it's making the difference. It's still taking us a good few clips before we finishes the first bit – it's only short and all.

Then he's saying how he's had enough and I has to clip him to continue. I has to admit, I'm doing it a bit harder then, so he's knowing it and he starting bawling dead loud, really laying it on you know and I gets Maggie coming butting in – shouting at us, yelling, so it's getting so I can't hardly think straight. But I puts her in her place – tells her how it's her fault, which is bloody right in all, and I'm telling her, reminding her, how I deserves a say. He's not just her bloody kid, he's my bloody kid and all.

It's then he sees a chance. He's ducking out then, nipping out round behind her. I'm not bloody having this. I knocks her out the way – no bloody problem – and I'm chasing after then, when he's dodging in the bedroom. And still he's ducking, diving, though he sees I'm trying to belt him – and he thinks he's seeing a way out – not a bloody chance – because I'm getting in the swing then, landing left and right, catching him a few times – he's got to bloody learn. I knows he's hurting now. I've got him in the corner, he's got no place to go, just crying out and saying, 'Daddy, Daddy don't hit us any more,' even tries it on with, 'Please.' Should have thought of that before. And I hears Maggies there and all, screaming in my ear. I feels its getting out of hand, like becoming all compulsive and I'm belting him some more.

Don't know what's happening then.

I'm trying to figure it in the car, after – when I'm sitting with the cops, because they're giving us a lift.

*

I has him squashed up in the corner between the wardrobe and the wall. I'm just standing, has hold of this bit of lamp. There's this blood I sees, spots of it, just specks, in a row, sort of line, going curving up the nets. The shade's coming flying off. I hears it bouncing on the window, and when it's dropping down and I sees it after then, hitting on the sill and falling off on the floor.

We has couple of them – two lamps, you know? They sits on these cabinets, Maggie has us make – just MFI jobs, dead easy when you knows how. We keeps them, one either side, top end, up by the bed. It's not the near one I has. It's still there, I sees it, hardly two foot off. I has hold of the other one I'm getting from the far side. It's sort of odd that. I don't remember I'm going round and I can't see us reaching over – need bloody arms – ten foot. It's seeming sort of a bit peculiar.

It's then, soon after, that they brings us down here – a few cops – two in the back, I sits between them in the car. They don't want to know. I tries explaining how its happening. How – if you thinks about it really – it's being bit of an accident. It don't interest them – not them – they don't want to hear. Just bloody ignores us – sticks a blanket on my head.

Bastard big sergeant's just the bloody same. He's leading us off, taking us in this cupboard room they has – has all fitted out with the photographic gear, even got the camera ready on a stand – one of them Polaroid, instant sort of things. He's taking a few photos – don't know if they're turning out – he's not letting us see.

I'm standing there anyhow, just like he's telling us and I'm trying to explain how it's starting, how I'm only trying to help. But he's being like before, just saying 'Shut it!' and grabbing hold my face, jerking round my head – nearly taking it off and using the flash then to get a photo sideways. Then when I'm stepping down, still doing exactly as he's telling us, he's pulling on my shirt and I'm pushed against a wall and he's standing really close, I feels his spittle on my face all the time when he's telling us, 'You want to learn to button it. No one gives a toss. You're scum of the earth you are.'

What way's that to talk to a bloke? He's bloody lucky I'm not nutting him.

What's he bloody know. He'll never make detective. I'm not scum of the earth. I got the headlines – I can prove it.

I lives with scum of the earth, so I bloody knows him, knows him bloody well. I lives with him until I'm ten. It's what they're saying in the papers when's he going down – saying in headlines, letters inches high. I got all the clippings.

They're saying it several times and in the Sunday papers after, because my mum's making a few quid telling what it's like, living with the Beast – Beast they calls him that time – BEAST OF BONAR LAW ESTATE. They has it all there – double spread, covering over two pages.

They're printing this big photo, showing mum and me, standing by this tree, just bit of a twig really, with the big wood support. They includes one of him of course, looking like a villain and this old one of my sister – mum's taking just before – where she's grinning at the camera and showing off all her gaps where her teeth are coming out. She's been a bit of an ugly kid. I never cares for her much. Never misses her at all hardly – because in the end – good thing about – it's getting rid of him. It's silver lining that.

The papers of course, they calls her pretty. They're calling my mum attractive. They mentions us in all, saying how I'm good looking – handsome sort of boy. They goes on describing us, saying I got these eyes – saying how they're sort of sad brown. It's a load of bollocks that. I got green eyes, always have had, so mum's always saying.

There's this one bit they're putting in a box – using thicker ink to emphasize – where they're telling how they goes out and about, asking round the estate and that. They never hears a good word. Everyone hates him, calls him bastard and allsorts – they just has to put dashes for some words they uses

75

– and everyone's agreeing if any bloke's scum of the earth, it's got to be him for definite.

Later, years after, when I'm older, under-age but going in pubs, I'm getting chatting with this bloke, who I'm remembering from way back and he's telling us how he's been doing time – same place and time as him. I gets to hear all about it then.

About how they keeps him all separate in this special part they has – segregates – just keeps him on his own with two screws who never talks. How they locks him in his cell, never lets him out, don't even let him have exercise – a turn around the yard. How when he goes to have his dinner the screws keeps him back, making him wait ages, because the other blokes want seconds. How they're bringing him down after, when the other blokes are finishing, and he's just getting to eat scraps – whatever they're leaving over. And the other blokes – because they knows he's coming then – they spits in it and allsorts and one bloke saves this turd and is dropping it in for him.

I'm hearing how on occasion – how the other blokes gets bored and takes trips down his part. How the screws knows what's happening – with finger on the pulse they're bound to – and how they're making themselves scarce, just giving it a few minutes. How when the blokes sees its all clear – like they're already arranging beforehand – a bunch of them nips in then and bungs this blanket catching him and covering him all over. How they has blokes dragging him down – holding him, so the other blokes starts beating him then. How they're using sticks and allsorts – big bits of wood and sometimes when their luck's in they finds bit of an iron bar and they beats him then until they sees blood soaking up and spurting – coming spraying out through the blanket. And all the time when I'm hearing I'm thinking how it's serving him – and the bloke and me are laughing and he's telling us how he's helping, always willing to help the deserving.

Then after, the bloke's telling us other stuff about him – about him sticking it only a few years, then he's taking off his trousers, using them to hang himself – found hanging in his

76

underpants – but I knows most of that already, because they're telling us it beforehand.

They don't mention it in the papers, I'm getting a few and checking them. Instead – we gets these coppers – coming round all sympathetic – barging in and telling us – staying on for a cup of tea. My mum, she's crying a bit and saying over and over, how he's been telling her all the time when she's visiting him – telling her – how he hates it. What's she want to see him for? Wouldn't have had me going. It's not bothering me – I was bloody glad to hear. Bloody good riddance. He was scum of the earth he was – every bastard knows.

Except for bastard coppers. Always bloody last to know. It's not bloody me – I got the headlines to prove it – should get their bloody facts right before they start accusing.

Never bloody listens. It's not as if I'm not trying to tell them – detectives and all – how it's happening – being bit of an accident, if you thinks about it really. I don't mean no harm. Starts off, I'm trying to help. Bunch of wankers – bloody clueless. Hardly takes an interest. Brings us down here – shoves us in – leaves us bloody hours – just bloody pisses off. Couldn't give us a cup of tea – too bloody much to ask. I gets no tea – no bloody tea – no bloody fucking matches.

I could do with a smoke and all. It's circumstances you needs one.

I mean, what kind of bastard gives you your tin, your tobacco and your papers, then says he's taking the matches for your own good. I been rolling anyhow.

GREGOR'S GARAGE

Ronald Frame

In the early 1960s our families were neighbours on a cul-de-sac, in an affluent suburb of Glasgow. We were all only-children.

My own parents were English, but already at eight years old – in kilt or tartan tie – I considered myself a Scot. Helen's mother was a widow, struggling with the upkeep of a Victorian house and also trying not to fall too far behind the fashions in the magazines.

Gregor's parents were supposed to have had a blazing row in Rogano's Restaurant, and it seemed that they could only shut doors in the house by banging them. Most often I glimpsed his father with his head buried in a medical magazine; I once found one of his empty whisky bottles sticking out of a beech hedge. It was said that the youthful Mrs Fletcher-Kiel had a separate account at the fishmonger's for flowers and sometimes gave lifts in her Citroen Ami to young male hitch-hikers.

Gregor knew precisely how much money was spent on him; he would tell us on the walks uphill from the prep school he and Helen and I attended. The more an object or item of clothing had cost, the less he liked it.

With just one single notable exception, that is – the one-seater, working scale-model of an Alvis convertible, fitted with a lawnmower engine and a set of bona fide, roadworthy white-wall tyres. He said the car was too 'dangerous' for anyone else to take the wheel, but that didn't stop *him* racing across 'Lindenwood''s sloping front lawn as fast as the engine, belching smelly black smoke, could propel him.

The Alvis was kept in a wooden construction like an over-sized kennel. Inside, there was just enough room for either the car – or for the three of us to huddle together, knees and elbows touching. Painted above the double doors was the incontrovertible mark of proprietorship: 'Gregor's Garage'.

We played as a threesome for no better reasons that I can think of now than physical convenience, a sense of exclusivity which the cul-de-sac encouraged with its high hedges, and also because the fact of our all being the same age seemed like some directive of fate.

I wasn't comfortable with Gregor's tight eyes, however, nor with the strength in his shoulders and arms. I was much more at my ease with Helen, who had inherited her mother's instinct for seeing the best in people – and an accompanying vulnerability which (without understanding so at the time) I suppose I wanted to protect her from.

As for myself: I spoke with an English accent, and at school I was considered abler than my age at arithmetic and composition. I tried to play down my scholastic ability sometimes, but I wasn't averse to using it as my trump card when I (mistakenly) thought that supplying answers to homework could help to make me better liked among the Picts.

I envied Gregor the Alvis. Speed gave him a rogue glamour. He drove the car faster and faster, and while Helen and I knew the stupidity of that, we were left on a perpetual knife-edge of excitement ourselves: would he overdo it one time and crash the thing?

He finally realized, though, that by not letting either of us ride with him, there were always going to be two camps: himself, and Helen and me. Whenever he drove past and saw the two of us with our heads together, as if we were in cahoots, his brow wrinkled darkly to a scowl. After that he would usually tire of the famously expensive car and suggest we do something else: climb a tree, or look for conkers, or play hide-and-seek.

Mostly we stayed in *his* garden – and, when it rained, sheltered in the summerhouse or the greenhouse. It was as if he didn't want to turn his back on the actual house itself and its mysterious life, in case it changed in some respect in his

79

absence. I would often see him looking, over our heads and past us, towards the windows and the shapes distantly visible through the shadows on the glass.

By an ironic coincidence Helen's favourite game was playing 'house'. Although he didn't like it, Gregor let her have her way. We would throw travelling rugs over the low branches of a tree or between two folding wooden clothes-horses. But he bored more easily with that than anything else, and if he lapsed into one of his moods he would kick at the clothes-horses until they collapsed on themselves. To me such behaviour was worse than rude, it was unforgivable: maybe Helen thought so as well, but I saw how his sudden violence thrilled her too, it made her eyes shine and her mouth almost smile, and all the more so when she begged him to stop, stop, stop, and he wouldn't, right leg thrashing away like a piston.

At school we were in the same class but sat in different rows and had our own confidants. Back in the cul-de-sac we were a trio, but sometimes awkwardly so.

One day I couldn't find Helen, and Mrs Monteith wasn't there to answer the doorbell when I rang it. I walked on to the Fletcher-Kiels' and up the gradient of gravel driveway. Something hit me on the back of the neck, and I looked up and saw Gregor in the fork of a tree, holding a fistful of chestnuts.

'Looking for your girlfriend?'

I was annoyed, but – even more than that – I was embarrassed.

'You're wasting your time, she's not here.'

'*You* told me,' I said, 'there weren't *any* conkers left.'

'Well, there are.'

'Yesterday you –'

'I've just found them.'

'They couldn't have grown in a day.'

'We're going out,' he called down in the drawly way his mother spoke, with which he terminated conversations, 'in ten minutes. To Killearn.'

'Oh well . . .'

I put my hands in my pockets and went back the way I'd come. On the potholed private road some sixth sense caused me to stop by the hedge and look in. Between the leaves and through the fretwork of twigs I was able to make out that the doors of 'Gregor's Garage' were opening: forearms and calves and knees and then a face appeared – Helen's – and I stood staring at the object she held suspended from one of her hands, a giant gleaming glory of a chestnut knotted on a string.

Helen didn't mention her private visit to me, and I was too proud and too afraid of a rebuff to enquire.

For a while after that – but only temporarily – Gregor seemed better disposed towards me. He made me a gift of some chestnuts: medium-sized and irregularly shaped. We had duels and he played as if he had a wager on his life. My conkers exploded like shrapnel. One day he asked me, very politely, to explain long-division to him, and I did, but when he couldn't pick it up and I shook my head at him as if he was a turnip-head he said Helen had told him that only this summer I'd wet my berth on the night-ferry to Denmark and that now he knew why I never let them see myself on a bicycle, because I hadn't the knack of getting up on to one with a crossbar.

I had meant those to be confidences between the two of us, Helen and me. Not the most awesome of secrets, but cautious offerings of trust.

I pictured Gregor's methods to myself, how he must have arm-twisted or hair-pulled them out of her.

Why, though?

It came to me in time, several years later.

Because he envied me, for those mental facilities he did not have himself. He wanted to keep me in childhood, frozen in that condition, when in fact a boy in our class already had the first dark tracings of a moustache on his upper lip and we all longed for our first day in uniform long trousers. He must have hated to think that anyone might speed past him, get 'there' – to puberty, to some acknowledged success or other, to wherever we were all bound in the future – before him.

*

Once I heard Helen's screams from my bedroom and I ran to look for her. Gregor's car was tearing round 'Lindenwood''s garden and there was Helen squatting on the bonnet, eyes tight shut and hands clutching the wheel arches.

I pursued them. For a few seconds I thought she was actually *laughing* through the screams. It was then that I flung myself at Gregor's shoulders. I wrested him out of the driver's seat and the car went somersaulting down the ramp of lawn. Helen was thrown off and in the process sprained an ankle and an arm falling. She started shouting at me from where she lay, and I couldn't understand why I deserved her anger.

'But it was *his* fault,' I said.

'*You* made us crash, stupid.'

'I only meant to help you.'

'Well, you *didn't*. You didn't at all –'

Her mother came hurrying up the gravel drive in high, sinking heels and a goatskin coat which even Helen, upright and trying to hobble on one foot, noticed and was disconcerted by. Gregor's father was found at last, and – doctor's bag in hand – he appeared, with his breath smelling sour, to attend to Helen. Gregor had managed to commando-roll clear and, unscathed, now stood staring at Mrs Monteith's breasts beneath her jumper, primed as they were like perky missiles in the siloes of a crossover bra.

When he was eleven Gregor was sent south, to Dorset, to a prep school that had a name for cramming. After that he was despatched to an illustrious public school near London.

In his teen years he would very rarely come home, if he still thought of 'Lindenwood' as his 'home' even. In the holidays he stayed with friends and their parents in ritzy foreign resorts, and took summer jobs crewing on yachts.

In Scotland, termtime lasted longer and began sooner, and early one September Helen said she'd been aware of being spied on – 'by guess who' – through a gap in the beech hedge as she walked home in the burgundy uniform of her Miss Jean Brodie establishment for young ladies. She told me about it the following day on the Milngavie bus out of town, and she didn't seem as unsettled by the incident as I thought she was bound to be. That year was the second last for both of us at our schools, and I observed how she was becoming much more her own person, with her own ideas and secrets: hiding her eyes behind a pair of very dark glasses on the bus journey home and causing heads to turn, pinning her skirt in at the waist after classes in such a way that she'd have taken a couple of inches off the length when she joined the chocolate-and-gold-blazered boys waiting at the bus stop on Great Western Road.

In Gregor's last year at boarding-school his parents bought him a Triumph Spitfire, and occasionally we would hear it between terms, disturbing the peace of the cul-de-sac at two or three o'clock in the morning. After he'd left school a rumour went about that he'd joined a motor-racing équipe; his mother denied it when she was tackled in the fishmonger's about her son's prospects, but later the very same week she made arrangements that all her shopping orders be delivered directly to the house in future, and indeed she was seldom again spotted by any of us walking those all too public thoroughfares of Milngavie.

After school, I embarked on an accountancy course in London, worked harder than I'd thought I would have to to get through, and more or less immediately landed a job with a big oil company. Several years down the line a more senior position fell vacant in their Edinburgh office and I was approached to fill it. I decided I had little to keep me in the south, and I accepted the offer.

In Edinburgh there were three years left to run on a company flat in the New Town, and I lived there in the interim.

Every second or third weekend I drove the fifty or so miles to Milngavie, and then the same back again. Quite by chance I happened to cross tracks with Helen, in a rhododendron glade near Mugdock Loch. She was walking her mother's cocker spaniel and I was walking my parents' Dandie Dinmont. Instantly her hands flew to her make-up, mine to my widow's peak of blowaway hair . . .

The dogs circled one another, and – conversationally – Helen and I adopted much the same ritual. She had modern good looks, I was thinking. Less a case of pretty-prettiness than a matter of attitude, a positive approach – colour-toning, highlighting this or that, a clean-cut Peter Pan hairstyle, a frankly determined straight nose and clear jawline. When she'd asked me to explain about myself and I had, she told me she was living in Glasgow, that she was joint-partner in a fashion boutique.

'It's playing at a job, really,' she said. 'But it did get me away from home. Barring Sunday dog-walking . . .'

We continued to meet after that, not by accident but by design. I was entertained to tea at her mother's a good few times, and I saw and heard how garrulous Mrs Monteith had become with the years. The talk was mostly of all the eligible men she might have married in the two decades since her husband's death.

As she listened, Helen's mouth would twitch at the corners with embarrassment and her shoulders grow tense. I knew she disliked the brazen romanticism of it all. I felt immensely sorry for her, and also nostalgic for the young woman who'd had to get by on little more than blithe hope and about whom I'd nearly forgotten during my time in London.

Eleven months after our re-encounter, and 'in a whirlwind' as her mother described it, Helen and I were married.

We made the necessary adjustments to the flat in Edinburgh, a very recherché nest in which to aspire to wedded bliss. But all too soon Mrs Monteith took ill – psychosomatically? – and we found ourselves returning to Milngavie more often than we had intended. Helen's mother and my own parents, conspiratorially or not, insisted on keeping for us each Tuesday's *Glasgow Herald*, with the pages of property advertisements awaiting our attention should we but choose to peruse them . . .

What happened next seemed somehow fated, or so we convinced ourselves at the time. The Fletcher-Kiels' old home in the cul-de-sac came up for sale. The current owners, a couple called Dawson, had let the garden get on top of them, and the house itself when we inspected it – seeing into all its once forbidden rooms – was only in so-so condition. The estate agent insisted it was too good a chance to let slip, and we hummed and hawed; at the same time Mrs Dawson took a particular fancy to Helen, who was pregnant, and she persuaded her husband – quite why, I can't say – that we were the only people who *suited* the house, it might even have been built for us. The upshot was that the offer we finally made, which was markedly lower than the agent's asking price, was the one the Dawsons accepted.

And thus, with such unexpected ease, the innocuous-sounding 'Lindenwood' became ours.

It took us a couple of years to make our own impression on the house. Likewise the garden required a lot of back-straining attention. But we achieved results in the end, and we had no regrets.

Sometimes at night, though, the house seemed to be dwelling on its own past, when the rooms – in the shadows of lamplight – became less our own; and when I'd scraped down and repainted the facsimile garage on the bottom lawn for our daughter Catriona's future use, not properly bothering that the dampness had warped and buckled the wood, it was impossible to keep the red letters of 'Gregor's Garage' from shining through my four, five, six layers of green emulsion.

I loved Helen very much, and often told her so, and especially now that she didn't work I stinted at nothing to provide her with every material advantage of which I could conceive. Occasionally, however, it was demonstrated very plainly to me that she felt overwhelmed by my solicitude, and even stifled by the comforts of our home. She would suddenly rise to her feet in the middle of a conversation, read her watch, and say it was time for the dog's walk, and it would be understood between us that my own company was not being sought.

She might be away for a couple of hours. When she came back, pink-cheeked, she invariably seemed in a better frame of mind, more reconciled to life, eager first to find Catriona and then content to let me kiss her welcome back. I fussed around her, made her something to drink or eat, stoked the fire as if to me the walk had been a small and intrepid odyssey.

Some evenings, however – unlike those when I watched her literally gasping for air – all she wanted by contrast was the privacy of the lamplight, the hush of our rooms, our distance in the darkness from prying eyes, the oh-so-familiar harmonies of domesticity.

'Look who's here,' Helen said to me, and she sounded quite displeased about his presence in the house. 'Gregor Fletcher-Kiel . . .'

It was a Sunday morning, and I had just returned from my elder's duties at church. In our sitting room I stood in my flannel business suit and shook hands, giving mine into his grip.

After thirteen years I wasn't able to recognize him. His nose was now Roman and patrician – a car crash on the track, he said – and his thinning black hair, cut modishly long at the back, was flecked with grey.

Helen's mouth, shiny with lipstick, was prim and narrow. She must have guessed, as I had, that he had been drinking.

'Thought I'd have a look at the old policies. You know?'

He smiled, charmingly and warily.

'Told the taxi driver how to come. God knows how many wrong directions I gave him. And buggeration, who do I find when I get here?'

It was our sixth year in the house, I started to explain –

'Snug as bugs by now, I expect?'

We listened to a brief but meandering curriculum vitae. We learned that he owned a sports car dealership in London (the 'West End') and Oxfordshire. 'Italian jobs. Dream cars. You know?' He said he might be looking for somewhere to open up in Scotland, since there was patently a gap in the market.

'Wouldn't you do better in Aberdeen?' Helen said – a little curtly, I thought. 'With the oil money?'

'Well, Aberdeen folk would probably come down here.' He spoke in an expensive, place-less, rather drawly accent – or absence-of-accent. 'And it's the oil people like *you* I'm after, Ronnie.'

Helen must have filled him in before my arrival. And only *she* ever called me 'Ronnie'.

I told him that that sort of transport was well out of my price range unfortunately.

'Too bad, too bad. Although this ole pile here must have cost you –'

Helen's mouth drew straight as he downed his whisky. (The best malt we had, I noticed.) Then she stared – very hard – at Catriona, who had just walked into the room: stared without blinking, almost as if it was a shock, as if she had completely forgotten about her and now certainly didn't care for her to see this specimen of adulthood. But Catriona quite happily turned her back on the three of us and left, running for the garden, for the green-painted hideaway beneath the trees we called 'Catriona's Den'.

'Could we get a car without a roof?' Catriona asked me some weeks later, eyeing what the company indulgently provided me with for appearances' sake.

'A convertible?' I said. 'Why would you want a convertible?'

She shrugged. 'I don't know.'

'I don't think they suit our weather very well,' I told her. 'Don't you like the car we've got?'

She stood at the window, considering but not replying.

'What would *it* say?' I asked her. 'If it could hear you?'

'I didn't mean –'

I thought I heard a crack in her voice. I held my arms out, for her to run into. I wrapped them round her waist and lifted her high.

'If we lived somewhere hot,' I said.

'The desert?'

'None of our friends has a convertible –'

Just as Catriona was going to speak, Helen appeared, soundlessly, at my shoulder. She put a segment of tangerine into Catriona's mouth, then another into mine.

'Before you brush your teeth,' she told Catriona, taking her from me and whisking her away. 'And so, sweet lady, good-night and let us off to Bedfordshire . . .'

I had a meeting arranged with some Americans from Aberdeen: in Perthshire, at Gleneagles Hotel.

I drove on there, foot hard down on the accelerator, after making a detour into Glasgow and dropping Catriona off at school. It was an instance of the more haste, the less speed, because when I reached the hotel, I discovered I'd quite inexplicably left the papers I needed at home.

I owned up, apologizing profusely. I said, it took seventy minutes to drive one way, should I go back? The Americans agreed, quite willingly. 'It's okay,' they assured me, 'we can get ourselves in a round on the Queen's Course meantime.' We had drinks first, then I took my leave of them.

Going back, I hit road-works just after Stirling and didn't reach Milngavie until nearly lunchtime. I parked in front of the garage doors and looked in the side window to check if Helen's car was there. It was, but it wasn't alone.

I'm an amateur when it comes to car-spotting, but a few weeks afterwards I found the model photographed in *Autocar*. A Ferrari, if I remember correctly, a Dino (was it?), certainly scarlet and indubitably roofless: although which manner of convertible it was, with which sort of hood – lift-off or fold-away – I would hesitate to say.

Luckily I'd left the papers in a presentation case in the vestibule, so I didn't have to venture into the house to look for them.

If Helen heard my arrival and departure she was never to say. Our sitting room was at the back (so she might not have heard), but our bedroom was at the front upstairs (so indeed she might). I purposely didn't look into my side-mirror or windscreen-mirror driving away.

That day as I tried to get up speed to overtake on the motorway, for the first time I was conscious that the car was underpowered. I kept slamming my foot down on the accelerator and revving, but it was a devil to get moving. I pressed the horn hard whenever my impatience got the better of me, which only rubbed other drivers the wrong way. I almost collided twice, and the escapes were close things. I think I wanted to cry but I was too angry. Perthshire had never before seemed so greenly, anciently indifferent to the sufferings we mere and callow mortals visit on ourselves.

*

Only once, maybe four months later, did Helen nearly give herself away.

She took a black eye. She told me – without looking at me – that she'd fallen against a door. Which door? I asked. She couldn't think at first. Her mouth had swollen up too, and I wondered if that was how Gregor preferred 'love' or whatever it was to him: by dispensing hurt and pain, as others bruise with kisses, and by denying himself the happiness he craved either because he knew he was undeserving or because he was afraid of making himself vulnerable to another human being and letting his heart speak.

Now we're honorary Texans, residents of our new home town, Houston. The oil money is supposed to have dried up, but the money-well never quite does.

My job boils down to representing the interests of a British conglomerate. As a family we enjoy – as the word is – 'enjoy' a rarefied existence, in a house with a twenty-five-yard indoor/outdoor swimming-pool, sunken jacuzzi-baths in three bathrooms, and a state-of-the-art white kitchen like an operating theatre. With a surgeon's skill Helen and I each excise with scalpel-precision whatever we wish to be absent from a conversation. Milngavie is seldom referred to; Catriona now talks with a mid-Atlantic twang, and is already – precociously – 'into' soft rock and muscular young tennis players.

The criss-crossing highways here are like a planet-scape, and I'm constantly amazed. I drive a mid-range Mercedes coupé, and Helen a souped-up BMW 3. But these roads are really made for the super-supercars, the dream machines. They're to be glimpsed now and then in a day, even faster than my Merc, outpacing Helen's matt-black toy. Maseratis, Ferraris, Lamborghinis. They move up on you undetected, like stealth-jets, they're there for an instant – and then they've gone, to wherever they're bound for: although I sometimes suspect their speed is for no true purpose, all they do is travel endless unvarying loops of glittering, twenty-first-century Houston.

I read recently, one of the big dealerships of European sports cars here is closing; they're going into powerboats instead, nothing priced at less than half-a-million dollars. The automobile business is now up for sale, the trade advertising is being pitched at those who will recognize its profit potential and – coincidentally – last week Helen told me that on the rich pickings from Mort's dental practice the Stavners are building a forty-metre pool for themselves with boulders and plants and an underwater sound system, so . . .

. . . so she's been a bit restless of late, taking her swimsuit with her when she drives off, eyes shaded behind her newest Persols, to investigate the construction work at the Stavners', who are almost our best friends in Texas. But I've noticed that she brings the costume back bone dry every time. I've noticed other things too, how on her return her gloss lipstick is perfectly in place and there's a faint trace of Scotch on her breath and she's still wearing her dark glasses as she gives me a quick peck on the cheek and goes through the house calling out – with a hint of urgency in her voice – our daughter's name.

THE CHLORINE BATH
Janice Galloway

Cold tile under the bare soles, shoeless now I looked. It was
cold altogether here, those blue gloss walls and chipped paint.
This cold white edge where my toes curled against the enamel.
I counted surreptitiously from the corner of an eye; colleagues,
from the shapes of their faces, the grim sets of the five mouths.
But there was a sense of oddness about the whole thing, more
than was apparent. This wasn't when we usually had time off,
not a permitted break in any sense. The way they were standing showed they knew it too. They were uncertain, steeling
against a kind of suspicion that didn't allow them to relax on
the rim beside me, the lip of this basin affair. It wasn't a basin.
No, more a sink, a deep sink and the enamel – was it enamel?
– pitted through to that mealy-coloured stuff underneath. The
wear and tear was smooth. Hundreds of footfalls to do that,
hundreds before us eroding the varnish shell of this bath with
repeated footfalls. Because that's what it was now I saw it
properly, squinting because I'd left my glasses somewhere. A
vast worm-coloured enamel bath filled with tinted blue water,
gaping like the mouth of someone drowned. I slid another
glance at the five beside me. My feet were cold, too free.
Shoeless. The shoes would be with my glasses and godknows
what else – hundreds of missing things probably. I just wasn't
prepared, hadn't taken care of half the things I should have
taken care of and could think of no good defence. You should
always be ready, in case. You must always be prepared. I
dared not look but suspected the others were barefoot too. It
is a tradition at the edge of water.

The wait went on.
 Still we did not look at each other.
 Maybe they didn't know what it was for either.

*

I knew it would not be good to ask. They were nervous too, smiling but without really meeting anyone else's eye, without meaning to smile only not being able to help it. I remembered reading that dogs baring their teeth isn't always what you'd think but is sometimes an indication of harmlessness, of lack of intention to attack. A lack of confidence it will make things any better. The room was thick with terrible hesitancy. It would have been good to leave but I couldn't. Something was crackling in the air like retribution about to strike, like a headache about to crack open. I could feel, in that terrible sinking of heart when the inevitable dawns, that our time was being wasted deliberately. I knew fully and absolutely it was the one thing I could be entirely sure of, the single unavoidable fact of the whole matter. We were having to wait for what in the end would be no reason at all. But I couldn't say that either. Making it plain would antagonize people and achieve nothing. Like them, I would have to wait and let the thing pass in its own time, go home soon afterwards, forget. Probably they'd reached that conclusion ages ago and I was the only one still working it out.

I felt stupid and helpless, not able to move for anger. My neck was stiff. And I was saying look there's no real harm in the situation, just in standing here, no real reason for anxiety, trying to keep my mouth shut and my nerves under control. Deep breathing made my chest hurt and spots appear on the mealy tile. On the fourth inbreath, a steady drip of liquid started to impinge on my concentration. It was coming from somewhere behind my back, louder and heavier, like boots across concrete. Something was wrong. I couldn't turn round. Then –

Mr Riceman appears at the side of the pool.

It dawns he could have been here some time, watching.

The grey face swoops at the corner of my vision before he stands in front of us and a loud snapping suddenly bathes the room in sound. My neck, unlocking.

We are turning round.

We turn round to look at Mr Riceman.

*

A ripple of white light, splintering. Through the hollow whispers of the bathing room, things begin to settle again, shapes re-emerging from the flow of broken colour. And we are no longer waiting. Something is about to begin. Everyone is far more relaxed than I had imagined. Peter rubbing his outer thighs, warming up for something and Colin and the woman whose name you don't remember, their arms crossed, share a joke you can't hear. The gold chain on her throat shifts as she tilts her neck, saying something soundlessly. Too quiet. The whole room is full of echo from nothing in particular, muffling everything else as though we are under water. She is laughing through this bubbling in my ears, her throat rising and falling. It's the only way to be sure she is making a sound at all. Colin's arms are bare. He isn't wearing a shirt. They look up. Maybe I was staring.

Mr Riceman coughs, making my ears pop.

The room opens up with drilling, children running, laughter from outside. And Mr Riceman speaking. That nasal edge to his voice, coming and going through the other noise. He is explaining our remit. Are we listening? It takes a while and no time at all to understand he is explaining in a foreign language, that the man is embarrassed. The remit itself is quite simple. We are to get into the bath. We are to get into the bath and sit together for the good of the department. He says it twice.

My jaw falls open.

He notices before I can do anything to hide it and glares.

Mr Riceman has grey eyes, like a spiked fish. The threat behind what he sees on my face, the danger I will be awkward, this is what he has been waiting for to be convinced that what he is saying is reasonable. He repeats it, this time in plain English with pauses to show he means business.

We. Are. Going. To. Get into. The. Bath.

No one breathes.

*

I suppose. Whoever issued the instruction. Knows. What they're doing. His decibel level increases unnecessarily. There is nothing else but Mr Riceman speaking.

Now. Let's. Not. Be. Silly. About this.
He looks us in the corporate eye.
It could be. A Good Thing. If we give it. A Chance.

There is a trace of a blush on his neck. I am on the verge of pity when he notices and, to spite me, decides to show the way. He sits on the rim, dipping his feet into the water. He is going into
He is in the water, flexing
his arms gently over the surface as though getting ready to swim, pretending he is at ease. Trying to make his movements less self-conscious. He has no shirt either. I try not to see his nipples, the black shape of swimming trunks beneath the surface that mean he was prepared to do this all along. The water flexes. Someone else moves in the water beside him: Peter, his face changing from regret to boyish enthusiasm, ginger down on his arms catching the light. He appears not to be wearing any clothes. I fight not to look at his crotch and fail. Natural redhead, brassy hair glittering at the rim of the trunks, flesh-coloured trunks with a red stripe. Natty. He bends his knees under the water to get as much of himself into the water as he can. It reaches mid-chest before he looks up, waving.
It's fine, he shouts. Better than you think.

You notice his wrist and think, He is wearing his watch in the water, knowing there is no use to tell him now when the damage has already begun. You watch him smile up out of the bath, ruining the delicate clockwork with the steady seep of chlorine beneath the glass face; you shudder at the thought that you are the only one who knows. He will lose that perfect smile if you speak so you stay silent, ashamed at your own need to pacify, not to be a cause of upset. Not again. Now the other woman, you can't remember her name though she has worked beside you for over ten years, the other woman with the gold chain glinting on her neck, drops the towelling robe.

She wears a black bathing suit, one piece, little patches of stretched skin on her thighs (you never thought to see her thighs before) from bearing children and she takes the steps one at a time, holding the rail you had not noticed before. There are three people in the water, only two remaining on the rim. Just the two of you. The other is a man who will do nothing to help you when the time comes. You think, I have no excuse now the others are behaving in this way. I will have to show myself to these people, let them smell the full extent of my weakness. You want to look down but you are dizzy with fear and the sudden stink of chlorine. You close your eyes again and think. It feels like a gown, a candlewick gown you had as a child and thought your mother threw out years ago. Your father made those cigarette burns on the cuff, not flattering, not even clean but something that covers. A covering for the snakebelly skin they demand you reveal.

Now.

There is at least a precarious safety now.

But soon they will expect you to undress and begin going down the steps as they have done. It will not be possible to refuse. They have complied. Anything less from you is merely being difficult. You shuffle excuses in half-sentences in your head and know that none will work. You know exactly what is expected, that nothing else will do. Trying to close your eyes is useless. The lids will not shut. It will not be possible to hide sight of anything in this room, impossible not to see or be seen. You have to be here, watching it all.

And Peter's hand is stretching out of the water, waiting for you to come to the edge, the woman rolling her eyes at your reluctance. Of course you are only being difficult. Mr Riceman, up to his waist, looks down that long nose as the bath narrows, forcing his people even closer together. Even closer. The smell of chlorine thickening, their skins not able to avoid touch. The cold kiss of goosefleshed other skin, the skin of other people ripples on your arms. They only want to touch. But you cannot stop the shivering, unable to speak, knowing soon you must act. Peter's hand opens. He smiles. The tiles are smooth as blades.

SWIMMING

Ian McGinness

Many who ought to know better say that the sea must claim
a certain number of human lives each year if it is to continue
to give up its harvest, as if the waters lived and had an appetite
for souls, or as if a crop of lobsters or herring, like corn in the
field, needed an annual application of blood and bone. Of
course, this is misty superstition. It is not to be taken literally.
But the deaths are literal, as is the fatalism which casts aside
life-preservers and ropes and passively accepts that the
supremacy of the sea must end in death.

Young Frankie Breslin was asleep when his father drowned.
As seaboots filled, as open mouth breathed water, a son lay
in a wooden cot, immobilized by tightly wound blankets.
When that green night obscured the low-slung sun, when the
solid world below the father's feet dissolved, his baby was
rocked before the fire as if on a gentle, tropical wave.

Frankie's mother was lucky. Her husband's body was found
on the rocks that night so she could bury him within the
appointed time. Other women had to wait weeks or months
for the bodies of brothers and fathers to turn up at the end of a
current: bloated, eyeless; reduced by crabs. When they pulled
Thomas Breslin ashore his pockets still contained his pipe,
tobacco in a tight tin, a sharp clasp knife, and threepence-
halfpenny in copper coins.

The boat was smashed, the lobster pots gone. Thus diminished, the Breslin estate consisted of a two-roomed house with
a thatched roof and a smoking chimney, a cow in-calf, one
donkey with cart in disrepair, assorted fowl, a fattening pig,
and six acres of bad land.

Once her husband's remains had been disposed of and the
worst of her public grief was over, Mary Breslin quickly came
to terms with the fact that she did not have the wherewithal

to keep herself and her children from starvation. As well as baby Frankie there were the twins, Kathleen and Clare: two years old and growing. Three young mouths to feed and no peace until they were filled. And those appetites would become more difficult to satisfy as the weeks passed, that was one certainty in the world. And they could not run naked as the beasts in the field. Something would have to be done.

Being a resourceful woman, Mary Breslin took action. Her late husband's uncle was in the position to lend her a small sum of money, and with this, the widow took the revolutionary step of opening a small shop from the kitchen of her home.

Under normal circumstances, this business would have been a failure. In the townland of Bracka there was no money to buy the packet cigarettes and chocolate and combs and razors with which Mrs Breslin stocked her narrow shelves. However, through a combination of history and geography and the politics of Empire, a large pool of customers had been provided for the fledgling enterprise. This came in the form of the three hundred and fifty six men who garrisoned the British fort and battery which guarded the entrance to the lough in whose waters Thomas Breslin had drowned.

The fort was one of a series built along the north-west coast in order to protect the Royal Navy's deep water anchorages on the Atlantic approaches. Someone, at some time, in some conference room in the War Office in London, had pointed a finger at an Admiralty map and his nail had tapped on the outline of the headland above the Breslin's home. Discussion groups had been convened, plans had been formulated, surveyors and engineers had been dispatched, until finally construction had begun. Now, overlooking the waters of the lough and the low peninsula to the west stood a collection of canteens, officers' quarters, stables, forges, workshops, stores, guardhouses, latrines, offices, armouries, kitchens, gun emplacements, and red-brick barracks roofed with corrugated iron.

The fort was surrounded by a ten-foot-high perimeter fence, but its main defence on the landward side was a deep moat quarried and blasted out of the solid rock of the promontory.

97

This moat ranged in depth from twelve feet to one hundred feet where the man-made obstacle ran into a natural chasm between two cliff faces. On the fort side, the sheer wall which rose from the jagged floor sprouted triangular metal supports on which was strung barbed wire which rusted in the salt spray and became hung with paper and scraps of dried seaweed.

Inside the fort, on circular emplacements high above stony beaches, atop cliffs where black-backed gulls nested and hatched their eggs, were four, six-inch naval guns. These ran on metal tracks and could be traversed through one hundred and forty degrees to command either the lough itself or the open sea. It was these which would deal with the threat of any aggressor, these which would watch over the Atlantic Fleet as it lay at anchor in the shelter of the twin-finger peninsulas in the war which was to come.

Three hundred and fifty-six men. If, each month, each man bought a packet of cigarettes or a box of matches or a shaving mirror then the Breslins would become the most prosperous family in Bracka. The fattening pig could become a sow, then another. An extra cow could be bought. Perhaps more land rented when the boy grew. Thick coats for Sundays. A new bed for the twins. Such dreams spring from a box of corn plasters.

Three hundred and fifty-six men. From Liverpool and Kilmarnock, Ballymena and Cardiff; Cornishmen and Ulstermen, Highlanders and Lowlanders; men from each and every part of the British Isles. But to the people of the townland they were usurpers, invaders; strange-tongued, uninvited: 'The English.' Here lay the difficulty for Mary Breslin, shopkeeper. Nothing is achieved without a price. For selling packets of boilings to young, child-like men from the back streets of the cities, Mary Breslin became, in the eyes of her neighbours, a 'soldier doll'. For selling tobacco and chocolate to men who had never heard a shot fired in anger, Mary Breslin was ostracized by the people of the townland to which her new husband had brought her four years before, people who would rather see her and her children starve in a state of nationalist grace.

And so Frank grew up in the small house below the fort in the company of his two sisters, his mother, and privates from the slums of Glasgow, corporals from East London, sergeants from the Norfolk Broads. The boy grew accustomed to uniforms but remained shy of these unusual men who tried to ruffle his hair and offered him sweets. He grew to recognize some of them; he learned their names and quietly welcomed their smiles, but then they would disappear and, weeks later, the boy would learn from pieces of conversation that they had been transferred to another battery or posted to a place which was only a sound. It was better not to expect too much from these strangers.

Less transient was a group of camp sergeants who were more or less permanently posted to the fort. The rulers of private empires in the stores, the offices, the workshops, the kitchens, they commanded great respect amongst the other soldiers, and were grudgingly tolerated by the people of the townland for whom they were an illicit source of bully beef, nails, biscuits, horseshoes, sugar, nosebags and custard powder.

Six of these sergeants called at the Breslin house every Tuesday evening, winter and summer. There was Graves, an armourer from Bristol. Two blacksmiths: Harcourt from Birmingham, McKay from Perthshire. Then there were Trump and Tallboy, small, pale men whose fingers were permanently stained with ink. Finally, there was Bowden from Gravesend in Kent, whose huge body seemed to have been hooped by a cooper; Bowden, who ruled the cookhouse and who smelled of bread and stewed tea.

Billy Bowden was a favourite with the children of Bracka. To them he seemed as a mountain: as tall as the tallest in the townland, broader than two potato-pinched men. His thick, black hair was swept straight back from his forehead, and from his top lip grew a moustache whose ends, sharp as a spear of grass, he greased and twirled. Sergeant Billy, as he was known to those who had no reason to fear him, would swing small boys and girls around his waist, holding thin wrists in his huge fists. With a casual flip he could catapult a child to his shoulders and, seated there, the favourite of the hour would bounce and yelp and hold the soldier's ears as a jockey draws the reins.

At eight o'clock these sergeants would arrive and Mrs Breslin would seat them round a table where already were arranged six glasses. When they had loosened their tunics and scraped their chairs closer together, Mrs Breslin would bring to them a bottle of poteen and place it in their middle, first wiping the bottle with her apron before setting it on the scrubbed wood in front of the fire. Bowden, for he was king of the kitchens and used to providing, would pour the clear liquid into the glasses, speaking each man's name as he did so. 'Mr Harcourt.' Harcourt would nod and lick a fold in the middle of his top lip. 'Mr McKay.' 'That's myself, sergeant,' McKay would say, his hand already enveloping the glass. 'Mr Trump.' Trump would be drumming his fingers on the table. 'Mr Tallboy.' Trump's twin would look round, as if another Tallboy existed in the room. 'Mr Graves.' 'Up to the top, sergeant. Don't be shy.' Finally, Bowden would pour his own measure and place the empty bottle on the flags at the foot of his chair. 'Here's to us, boys. Defenders of the realm; the backbone of the army.' They would drink, some in one violent gulp, others in two or three throws, then replace their glasses on the table and light their tobacco.

'You wouldn't have another bottle there, Mrs Breslin?' Bowden would ask after a few minutes of contemplative silence, and Mrs Breslin would rise from her dark corner and wipe the bottom of another bottle drawn from the sack at her feet.

After the third bottle, there would be no more silences between the men. In air thick with smoke from pipes and cigarettes, the conversation would develop from an analysis of the petty politics of the fort to talk of letters from home and the detritus of civilian life. After the fourth bottle, grievances tended to be aired and plans laid to rectify wrongs in the administration of the British Army. After the fifth bottle, Trump and Tallboy would fall out over some imagined slight; McKay would dream of life as a gamekeeper in Perthshire; Graves, sweating, face reddened, would become the landlord of a country pub. And as Harcourt's eyes moistened at the thought of his poor, dead mother, Bowden would sing in his deep booming voice songs of Kent and the country and the life of an army man.

The sixth bottle was always the last. It was usually a solemn affair because the sergeants knew the evening was at an end and that they must soon start on the short road back to the gate: under the bright, frosted moon; through the sea mist; soaked by rain wind-blown from the mountain; crunching through the bright, white snow; massaged by the still, smooth-black night.

As the last drop was drunk the men would stretch in their chairs before rising and buttoning their uniforms. Trump and Tallboy would stumble and push each other out of the door. McKay would salute their hostess; Graves would look back longingly at the last empty bottle reflecting the light from the fire. Harcourt would begin to speak but would stop as his eyes filled again with tears at the sight of a mother. Only Bowden would exchange words with the woman of the house, thanking her for her hospitality and discreetly sliding coins on to the table beside his glass. Mary Breslin would make a combination bow and curtsy and rub her fingers on her apron; silent as ever, she would look at the floor rather than at the man or the money he had left behind.

If Frankie was still awake he would be sitting on the milking stool in the shadows below the darkened window. He was allowed to remain in the room while the men drank, unlike his sisters who were put to bed half an hour before the sergeants arrived. Clare and Kathleen were easily excitable and had not learned to be properly modest: they pestered Bowden for swings and lifts and shoulder rides, and pulled at the buttons on his tunic. Young Frank was different: he could sit still for hours listening to the songs and stories, being washed in those strange accents.

He studied the movements of the men, especially those of Bowden. The big Kentishman's gestures emphasized power and confidence: pulling McKay's head towards him and whispering in his ear; gripping Harcourt's arm in his fist while making a point. Then singing, eyes closed as if immune to the reactions of others, hands resting palm down, light and steady, as if feeling for a pulse. Sergeant Billy could rest his elbows on the table and dominate the others by leaning forward to shadow them like a threatening cloud. The muscles would move in his upper arm, wrinkled in khaki or bare after the fourth bottle, thick as the boy's waist. He would amplify his emotions with reference to his moustache. When relaxed and happy he would stroke the growth gently, sweeping the body down then upwards towards the ends. When annoyed or impatient, thumb and forefinger would grip the points and violently twirl them until it seemed that the hair must cork-screw from his face. Silently, unseen, Frankie would feel on his own bare lip and twist in time with the sergeant.

Before he left the house on those Tuesday nights, Bowden would always search out Frankie in his usual seat in the shadows. He would stand over the boy, smiling, swaying slightly, then draw his hand from his pocket and flip a coin in the air, laughing when Frankie caught it in mid-flight. The boy did not usually accept anything from the soldiers of the fort, unlike many of the other Bracka children who would pester for sugar and sweets. His mother had taught him pride. He should not dance and caper for what the Englishmen had to give. But he took Sergeant Billy's coins. He felt it would be cruel to refuse this man. 'One for the potboy,' Bowden would say as the copper coin left his fingernail with a whir, a ring, catching the flames as it spun. Frankie would hold the money in his closed fist and wait for Bowden to say more but the sergeant would only smile again and belch and leave the Breslin's home with a wave and a slight stagger.

Frankie kept this money in a glass jar in the room off the kitchen he shared with his mother and sisters. He did not spend any of it but counted it out on the bed on Sunday mornings before Mass, arranging the coins in rows, in circles, in crosses on the grey blanket. They were his troops, he was their drill sergeant. He gave orders: formed, then reformed the company; wheeled and turned. He exerted his will, marched his men through the valleys, over the hills, across the rivers of loose wool, before they returned to their transparent barracks to await the next reveille. And each Tuesday there would be a new recruit: usually just a soldier of the line but sometimes a fat, heavy penny, like a large Kentishman in uniform. Occasionally, on special days, there would be a thin, silver sliver like an elegant captain in braid. But despite the presence of the shining officers, a solid, weighty sergeant always led the troops, in column or line, in fighting disposition or on parade, until the bells sounded and the bodies were swept up by a giant child's hand and funnelled back into camp.

It was on Sundays that the men from the fort swam in the sea water of the lough. Frankie watched them from high on the rocks above the house as they paddled and floated and lazed and sported and dived. Most used the white strand over the brow of the hill, an arc of bright sand which lay beneath the heathered, sheep-spotted slopes of the mountain. These were the summer swimmers, those men who stayed in barracks when the rain fell or when the temperature required the addition of a coat. Another group avoided the beach and instead dived from the rocks which extended into the sea from the shingle beaches below the cliffs. These men swam on every Sunday in the year, regardless of the weather: serious swimming, not the splashing and flopping to be seen on the white strand from where, on fine still days, the hoots and shouts could be heard until early evening.

Many of the all-weather group were large, well-covered men who assumed a smooth grace when sliding through the green water off the rocks. Their exercise was shorter in duration but more intense, involving long, individual swims out into the waves and currents of the deep water towards the far peninsula. With varying degrees of elegance, they would dive into dark pools between the volcanic fingers which stretched from the bottom; surface, blowing hard, then strike out in a slow crawl or bobbing breaststroke round their favourite course. In summer, these swims would be followed by a brisk rub then a smoke on a sun-warmed slab above the tide. In winter, the bodies would emerge, smoking, from the water and the men would quickly dry and dress before walking back to the fort and a mug of cookhouse tea before the hot stove.

Bowden was a winter swimmer. His stripped body was

broad and fleshy like John Joe's two-year-old white bullock, although the legs he stood on looked too thin for such a size of man. Before the plunge, he exercised on the edge of the rocks, whirling his arms round his body: first the right, then the left, then both together, until it seemed he must overbalance and topple into the sea like a broad-bellied, flapping gull shot from its cliff nest. Frankie, used to the smack of stones in pools, wondered at how such a big man could dive into the water and make so little noise, so little impact; leave barely an impression apart from bubbles and ring-ripples which soon lost themselves in the weed tangling tide-surge. Emerging after the dive, Bowden embraced the waves, dragging foam and the fat, glistening swell towards, then behind him, moving calmly, in control, casually spouting water from his mouth. And on the cliff tops, the Sunday dressed people of the townland watched and shook their heads, then turned their backs on the sea and these men who bobbed like seals as the bell sounded for Mass; these men who ignored the call of God's dry land.

As he floated on his back after the exertions of the first swim, Bowden's eyes would look up towards the hill and the small, silent spectator who attended the exercise each week. Sergeant Billy would call to Frankie but the boy did not reply. He would invite Frankie in for a swim but the boy remained on the little rock with mossy footstool where he perched under the sun and rain. One of the men might make a joke and the others would laugh. 'Paddy's got stones in his pockets,' he might say, and the others would splutter in the water. And then another, 'Paddy's got lead boots.' But Frank didn't mind because he could not hear the words, only the laughter, and the laughter made him feel somehow closer to the sea.

One hot Sunday in the summer before Frankie's ninth birthday, the boy appeared as usual on the hill from where he could see the beach and the rocks. Bowden dived, swam in the sea with the others, then hauled his water-drawn body up on to the warm shelf where the men stored their clothes. He towelled dry his skin and the dark hair which lay flat and sea-glistening in the sunlight. As he stretched and felt the air warm him, the sergeant looked round and saw the small figure in the distance. 'Come on down for a dip, Frankie.' The boy seemed closer than was normal. 'Come on, lad.' Frankie took a few steps down the hill. 'That's it, son.' Bowden stopped drying himself and with his toe nudged a fellow swimmer who was basking in the heat. 'The little bugger's coming. Would you believe it.' Frankie came nearer. 'Come on, son. Nearly there.' Now several of the soldiers had stopped swimming and were watching the boy's approach. 'Good lad.'

Frankie stood before the sergeant, not stretching as high as the big man's navel. He had stripped and stood shivering in a pair of underpants his mother had sewn that spring from a fifty-six-pound flour bag. Bowden's arm rested on the boy's shoulder and they both stood facing the deep water. 'What do you think, son?' The other soldiers had stopped swimming and waited, watched. Frankie was trembling. Bumps rose on his skin. He took a step back but was restrained by a large hand pressing against his back. 'Only one thing for it, lad. It's what my dad did to me when I was younger than you.' Frankie must have guessed what he meant because he tried to spin from the man's grasp but it was no use: the sergeant had him, lifted him, threw him up and out, and in a tangle of arms and legs the boy plunged in a land-animal crash into, under, the water, the bubbles, the silence; the heart-bursting, lung-bursting fear.

Young Frank rose towards the light and blindly gulped in air and water. He felt himself sink once more and struck out with arms and legs until one foot came into contact with something soft and vaguely warm, and he felt hands grip him and hold him close and safe.

On the Sundays that followed, Bowden taught Frankie to swim in the green sea off the rocks. But the boy did not learn to like the water. He did not assume the ease of the men who swam beside him. For Frankie, this was not sport or entertainment, but a battle against an enemy. He felt he had not been constructed for this medium. Those small feet were happier on earth.

When Frankie swam, he did so in a frantic, nervous manner, with his head pulled back as far out of the water as his neck would allow. He felt nothing below his body except drowning and a black, airless descent. As he splashed through the sea his eyes were fixed on the closest point of contact with the solid world, and on the final stroke he grabbed for rocks, for weed, with a clawing hand. Sergeant Billy laughed and told him to relax, to accept the support of the water. But Frankie felt the water pull him down. Bowden told him to float with his head towards the sky. But Frankie felt that if he ceased to struggle the sea would suck him under.

The weeks of that dry, hot summer passed. The Breslins lived their lives unnoticed and at night went to bed under the lights of the fort. On Tuesdays, the sergeants drank in the kitchen and spoke of the same women, the same places; the same futures, the same pasts. Frankie's army increased in size and went on manoeuvres each Sunday morning before Mass.

Frankie continued to attend the swimming sessions but only occasionally did he join the men in the sea. When he did decide to swim he would first stand shivering on the brink, then lower himself inch by inch until only his head was above the water. Hanging on to a rock, he would dip up and down, teeth chattering, then launch himself on a brief, splashing excursion along the edge of dry land until victory was re-established. As the others continued their exercise, the boy would climb up on to the rock ledge to dry himself on Bowden's towel, dress, and take up guard over the men's clothes and boots.

In early September of that year, at the end of the month's first Tuesday, Bowden spoke to Frank in the kitchen which smelled of tobacco and poteen and soldiers. The sergeant looked round conspiratorially and leaned down, breathing alcohol. 'Don't you go to the rocks this Sunday, young Frank.' The boy looked up anxiously towards the man. Bowden laughed then hiccuped. 'Don't worry, you've not been dismissed the service. No.' Sergeant Billy looked over his shoulder again, enjoying this pretence at secrecy. 'You come down the beach where the other men swim. There's something special on this week and I want you there to bring me luck.' Bowden pulled his hand from his pocket and flicked a coin in the air. It spun heavily and Frankie caught it, his top hand slapping shut on the bottom like the jaw-snap of a dog. 'You come down early, mind. You're my luck, boy.' Frank lifted the upper hand and on his palm saw a fat, round shilling: a dramatic addition to his army: a colonel at least. Bowden winked and turned to go. 'Plenty more where that came from. After Sunday. Remember, young Frank. You're my luck, boy.'

That Sunday was long in coming but when it came Frankie woke before his mother and silently slipped out of the bedroom into the kitchen. As he dressed he felt the silver shilling heavy against his leg: it had not yet joined the other recruits in the glass jar. It seemed too special for that.

A light wind blew and dispersed rags of mist over the sea. At that early hour there was the first chill of winter in the air but that would be gone by the time the sun rose above the hill. Boats were drawn up on the white strand, some containing a tangle of nets. A sole cormorant skimmed over the wave tops while above, two young, dirty-grey gulls stumbled and soared in the warming breeze. As Frankie chinked his way through the pebbles which sloped above the sand, a pair of oyster-catchers rose and flapped above his head, shrilled abuse, flashed black and white wing stripes at the intruder. The boy was alone under his own sky. He gathered his jacket close round his body and curled to sleep in the lee of the boats.

He was wakened by the call of the gulls and the sound of boots on pebbles and the talk and laughter of Englishmen. Startled, he pulled closer into the shadow of a boat and looked out into the clear day lit by early morning sunshine. A great many soldiers were gathering on the beach but they were in uniform, not dressed for a swim. There were many strangers among them but Frankie recognized some faces from the shop, and also the men who drank in his mother's kitchen. All of the sergeants were present, all that is except Bowden, the man who had ordered the boy to the white strand.

Frankie stayed still and quiet and watched as the men talked in groups and skimmed stones on the water. Some smoked and flicked their cigarette ends at the scavenging birds; two young privates wrestled, kicking up the dry sand.

They seemed to be waiting, waiting like the boy under the boat, waiting for Bowden.

A man shouted. Frankie could not hear the words but the men fell silent and turned and looked away from the sea. Some stood back as if clearing a space. Legs stood near Frankie and through them he saw a rowing boat being carried down to the water's edge, and bare skin strangely coated, and a jumble of khaki pushing and straining behind. Then a voice: 'Has anybody seen the boy? I need my luck with me today.' It was Bowden.

Frankie crawled out and pushed his way through the legs until he reached the clear space in the middle of the soldiers. They did not resist his progress but urged him forward with their hands. He broke through the final line and there, alone in the circle, was Bowden. But it was not the Sergeant Billy the boy knew from before. This Sergeant Billy wore a tight, smooth cap which fitted his head like skin, and his body was draped in what seemed like a woollen cape. He gestured towards the boy, while at the same time feeling for the fastening at his neck. 'Good lad. I knew you would come for Sergeant Billy. Now we can get on with it.'

Bowden let the blanket slip from his shoulders on to the sand and stood before the crowd, naked apart from a new swimming costume. The men murmured, some breathed in sharply, for covering every inch of Bowden's skin was a thick layer of what appeared to be white lard. The sergeant stood before the soldiers and turned slightly, as if for examination. Frankie heard the swallow of a man behind him. Even the gulls fell silent.

'Ready for the oven, sarge?' a voice shouted from the back of the crowd, and the men laughed and the tension was broken.

Bowden put his head back and laughed with the others. 'I'll cook your goose when we get back to the fort, Weller, don't you worry about that.' The men laughed again.

Bowden walked down to the water's edge and the crowd followed. Now there was an air of celebration about this outing and Frankie was being swept up in the excitement without understanding what was unfolding.

Still facing dry land, Bowden stood in the shallows and

extended his hands. Sergeant Harcourt ladled grease from a tin into the cupped palms and Bowden smeared the stuff over his face and neck, completing his basting. Then he called Frankie to him and, lifting the boy in his arms, turned to the sea. Frankie could smell lard on the man's skin, he could feel heat radiating from the man's body. 'That's where we're going, young Frank.' Bowden pointed. To the waves. Further, across the greenness. Out, past the sandy bay, beyond the rocks. Into the distant water below which lay crushed boats and drifting pots; far, far from land to the beaches of the twin peninsula which lay low beneath the hills in the distance. 'Will you help me, boy?' Frankie nodded, forgetting the crowd, seeing only this man's eyes.

The rowing boat was launched and five men scrambled aboard. Bowden swung Frankie high over the gunwale and into the arms of Sergeant McKay, who smiled and patted the boy on the shoulder. Graves threw Bowden a pair of goggles. The crowd moved closer to the waves. Voices raised from a murmur to a roar. Bowden waded into the water. The soldiers began to cheer. Bowden's shoulders dipped beneath the silky swell. Trump and Tallboy ran splashing through the surf. Bowden began to stroke and hats flew in the air. Shoulders and head broke the surface as he breathed, deeply and evenly. The boat cut along, guarding, protecting him. He could hear the men. 'Bowden! Bowden! Bowden!' And at his side, from above, a small voice: 'Do it, Sergeant Billy, do it.'

The cold bit into Bowden's chest and chilled his legs, but he felt strong as he struck out for the far-off shore.

WALLY DUGS
Candia McWilliam

When she put her hand in the peke's ruff of silky blonde hair, you'd only to think of her lifting the wee dog up to her old head and pulling the thing down over it like a wig to get some notion of what Grisel Carnegie had looked like when she had been the prima ballerina *assoluta* of Esme Stewart's heart. Now you could see her skull's shifting plates through the spun-up hair, and as she chewed, there was a clicking sounded like a frog looks when it swallows down some midgey morsel. She took her lunch in by degrees, making dolly meals on the fork and then edging it up to her mouth, avoiding her nephew's eyes when she actually snapped and swallowed. Beauty was ever ill-served by the act itself of eating. Esme had loved her little appetite, saw it for an expression of that sweet passivity so light and downy and otherwise unimposing in a ladylike woman, a woman with whom you would be proud to be seen and with whom you need never converse save anent that which was pleasant. Esme had been an advocate, lovely on his feet in the court, Grisel imagined, as on the dance floor, with his long robe making much of his gestures, the little wig not undignified but proper to his office. She had naturally never witnessed him as he strode and ranted and dealt out fiery justice in the court. But he was well spoken of, she remembered that, and she could still, all these years later, induce people to mention him, frequently favourably, and that was like a sip at sugary tea. She was a sipper, never wishing immersion in sensations. Those sips did her fine, as they always had.

Glenbervie was not a Home. It was strange how unreassuring the word home could become once you were older. Anyway, Glenbervie wasn't, so that was all settled. As a matter of interest, Ailsa and Carl had looked around a

considerable number of Homes before deciding that Glenbervie, a warden-supervised sheltered development, would be
superior in every respect. She'd a patio, a hot plate for keeping
dishes warm when she'd guests, a terrific view of the whatname hills and a button to get through to the warden all hours
of the day. And night, but she could not imagine having the
bare face to use it. Ailsa visited a bit less now because the
baby was walking and she said she didn't trust her around
the trinkets, she'd never forgive herself if Rhona smashed a
piece in the famous china collection. Grisel had a lifetime's
aviary of china birdies, all up on the sliding-front cabinet
where she kept the glasses with the capitals of Europe written
on them, with a landmark on too, that tower for Paris, a ruin
for Rome, and a guardsman for London. Madrid had had a
bull as she remembered but it was long broken, not in the
move to Glenbervie but at some fairly riotous gathering where
a hem had caught the glass and sent it flying. Skirts could do
that then, sticking out and solid with net and Vylene, full of
starch as an ashet of mashed potatoes. They were becoming
though, to anyone with a dancer's bearing, like herself. The
stiff skirt would encircle its wearer like a big flower, making
her little legs just wavy stamens among the rustling petals of
petticoat. You'd to crush the skirt to yourself at night in a car,
both to get in and so as not to impede visibility. The rustling
petty was right up there with a life of its own misting up the
windscreen and rising like boiling sugar to fill the side windows before you knew it. The way to control those skirts,
Grisel Carnegie knew, as the girl who had broken the glass
with Madrid and maybe a bull maybe a cow on, had not
known, was to furl them like an umbrella, the way a bindweed
flower is turned on itself before its first time of opening, the
time after which it just flushes up in colour then falls limp like
a thing forgotten, a hankie maybe. To furl up your skirt you
stood with your hands by your side and turned your hands
against your upper legs as though you were twisting the top
and bottom of yourself in two at the waist. The bell of the
skirt followed naturally. It was like that with garments. You
either did or did not know how to make them do as you
wished. Grisel could honestly say she had never known her

clothes step out of line. Gloves had remained wed to each other, her appropriately treed shoes had not pinched, and no button had ever broken with its hole.

She'd not been young either when she had favoured those big skirts like flowers, but she had taken good care of her appearance with the result that she'd the waistline younger women had lost to the reproductive urge. Not that old, mind, but approaching an age about which to be discreet. Esme had understood that, of course.

What age Esme had been Miss Carnegie did not know. She could have made enquiries, there were plenty of folk must have known him at school and then at the University, but she preferred a little haziness, a little of what she liked to refer to as romance. The more veils it dons the closer romance sidles to untruth, but Grisel was for beauty over truth, fortunate, perhaps, when all was said and done, at Glenbervie.

The china birds were cast in attitudes, the attitudes of real birds, which no real bird will hold for longer than an instant. The effect of many colourful frozen creatures, shiny, without the softness and blur of feather, tapping a coy ceramic snail or arrested on a frosty twig, was lightly deathly. The birds were demanding when it came to dusting, more demanding than one living bird might have been about its seed and water. But Grisel had forsworn living pets when she left her Pekingese with Ailsa and Carl.

'Taking that dog, it's like a matrimonial visit,' Carl would tell Ailsa when he got home. God, he was pleased to get home, too. You never knew the meaning of the word 'home' till you'd been to a place like Glenbervie for the best part of a day, including the drive. 'She holds on that tight to the bloody dog' – he set it down now on the coir matting in their front hall – 'and it has nothing at all to say to her and looks guilty and embarrassed and desperate for a cigarette.'

Neither of them disliked the dog that much or they would not have relented about having it put to sleep when the warden at Glenbervie explained that dogs were not ideal for the ambience of the residential complex. The baby weeded at the dog's rich coat for hours, and kissed its squashed face. The Peke permitted liberties from the baby it would have bitten off at the knee in anyone else. Indeed, the dog's and the baby's size, gait and expression were increasingly similar: each could look outraged or appealing, each was prone to soon-forgotten rage. But the animal would keep its glamour as young humans rarely do, although baby Rhona was one of those changelings who astonish by their dissimilarity to plain parents, so dog and baby were a strange, bewitching pair, fraily matched for the time being.

Once Carl had his drink and Ailsa was sitting over from him on the other sofa with the dog and the baby in a tangle at her side making, it had to be admitted, a regrettable state of the sage velvet stripe, he began his story of the day. The way to tell it was to save the marrow in the bone till the end, to worry at the tale until it split and the nourishing part was there at last. For Ailsa, so certain of her own freedom from dependence – even upon Carl, who was after all only a man – the cream of the joke was always Esme, how he came in to the fortnightly encounter of her husband and her aunt-by-marriage as they sat in the sheltered chalet in the shadow of the whatname hills surrounded by china birds and pecking at food intended as festive and failing in that intention, an inch of fish here, a jot of jelly there, and lashings of Carnation milk for a treat. The Carnation came in a lovat green earthenware jug marked 'Brora'. Not that she'd been any of these places, the old coot, but it did make present-giving simple enough. Just keep your eyes peeled for a place-name and snap it up. Sensible un-dependent Ailsa had no patience for bits and bobs, it was like clothes, a waste of time and money just to give yourself allergies with the dusting or, in the case of clothes, acute discomfort. Ailsa favoured the untailored, the non-iron, the elasticated.

It was appalling to see how Grisel still kept all that nonsense up, with her assisted hair and the kitten heels to her old lady's shoes. Surely she could shut down on her appearance now? She'd been playing that tune all her life. Might it not be a relief to change stations? Tune out of being feminine, tune in to feminism maybe. Ailsa loved her feminism, it was so dependable a comfort. She knew she would cope fine if Carl was inconsiderate enough to leave life before she did. She was a natural coper, so she thought. She knew what was what, she often said, only very occasionally acknowledging the disappointed voice within that asked if this was it, was there nothing more, nothing along the lines of what she sometimes glimpsed in her sleep or heard in music or flowing water, a sheen in the air.

Carl was spinning out the drive, making it all as boring as possible, partly to make Ailsa feel bad but also, she hoped, for they were not on bad terms, to whet her appetite for any fun to come. 'So eventually I get off the A9 anyhow and cruise down to the Alpine Village itself. Usual smell of rubber briefs and grey potatoes and a wee dab of cologne for the Sabbath. I'm dying for a drink, of course.'

She knew what to ask. 'Gay Paree? Romantic Rome?'

'It was London this time, and a sherry. She must have laid it in for me. Mobile shop service looking up.'

'Just the one?'

'Two out of her and one solo in the kitchen.' That'll be five in all, thought Ailsa.

'She serves out the dinner slow so it's cold on those ferocious hot plates and sizzling but chilly, the Brussels still frozen at the middle and smelling like cats on the outside. I put Carnation on the mashed-potato balls just for some variety. Christ, have me put down by the time I'm old, will you not?'

I will, Ailsa thought, don't worry. Illness had no place in her understanding of the world. But I, she continued in her strong mind, intend to live for a long time after you are gone, and always to be myself and do as I will. It did not occur to her that she might ever become an old lady in a colony of old ladies, cooking bland food for ungrateful connections, and shopping from a van full of tins. She would be splendid, and wilful, and eat garlic. No one would discuss her after visiting her save with admiration.

'Yellow jelly?'

'Red jelly.'

The baby tried to copy her parents, 'Ledlellylellylelly.' The parents dismissed this primitive vocalizing. The dog jumped down off the sofa one end before the other, it was hard, beneath the hair, to tell which, and shimmered over to the fireplace. There was no fire in the grate but a white paper fan, made anew by Ailsa annually to fill the fire basket in the summer months. She was good with her hands, undomesticated but stylish.

The baby followed the dog to the fireplace with the vehemence of reunited love. The two, dog and baby, big-eyed, snubnosed, took up their places before the empty fire. It was not yet dark outside, the city had not settled down beneath its skyline. Carl made to get another drink. Ailsa took his glass from him. In the pocket of his jacket was the remains of a packet of dry roast nuts he'd got at the filling-station. He tipped the lot into his mouth while Ailsa fetched the new drink. She made it weak. It wasn't so much the health side of his eating and drinking that bothered her – what would be would be – but she was put off when he had overmuch to drink. He grew slobbery, asking for reassurance, even declarations. To make up for the weakness of the whisky she caressed his neck when she returned and pretended to be more interested than she was in his relating of the day at Glenbervie. She concentrated with the top of her mind on recollecting, detail by detail, the living-room of Grisel Carnegie; the rest of her mind she allowed to swim. She didn't need a drink to find an easy drifting movement to her thoughts. Unadmitted dissatisfaction had given her a talent for dreaming that she would have denied utterly. But the truth was that alongside her marriage to Carl and the tiring business of having Rhona, she ran dreams in her head like films without end. Their matter was not dramatic, but softly eventful. She was not a heroine but an object of curiosity, even longing, to unspecified, unnamed creatures, perhaps not even men. The glow of anticipation and undisturbed aftermath was the climate of her lower, denied, dreaming.

What Carl and sensible Ailsa could not take about his aunt was the way she made of her eventless life a romance, as though that life had been enough for her. It was a way of rationalizing a totally pointless existence, they agreed. The titivation, the unconsummation, were all part of a sickness which only in recent years had been shaken off by women, that much was obvious. Now women not only knew what they wanted, but went after it and got it, not like Grisel with her net petticoats that had netted nothing, and her silent china companions and dreams of a man who'd lived with his mother and gone to dancing classes in his fifties. Illusions, breakable illusions, was all Carl's aunt had, he thought. Look at Ailsa, now, she'd never wander like that in her thoughts, yearning for something nobody could put a name to. He prided himself in knowing what was in Ailsa's wee mind, he really did. Like now, he knew it would be the room at Glenbervie, the flock of motionless birds.

Beneath that picture, which was indeed in Ailsa's mind, hovering at the surface of it, something stirred and fluttered, never quite roosting. The texture of her dreaming was light but dense, like a field of high flowers, like a net in slow water. Something was approaching her, something wonderful, over the meadow, through the water.

'I gave her the dog to hold and she held on to it as usual like grim death and it pulled its wally dug face. They looked up at the china dogs, one either side of the mantelpiece, their snub noses, big eyes, painted whiskers, unbearably appealing pathos. Each dog had a clownish sorrow to its face. The baby and the living dog played below the china dogs, the pleated white fan behind them in its fire basket. The two were staring into each other's faces, seeming to grow more alike as they stared. On the mantelpiece the china dogs made a quaint guard for the drift of invitations and reminders ranged along the mantelpiece. Carl and Ailsa were a busy couple. It was unthinkable that they would be halved, one half or the other bereft. Death wouldn't get an appointment squeezed in, their schedule was that busy.

'She's ageing fast, now. The winter might just do it.' Carl was realistic. Everyone had to go sometime. They'd put the dog down then with an easy conscience. Rhona would for certain be too young to notice.

The baby gave up the staring match and grabbed the dog by both ears to pull its face to hers. The pair kissed and began to roll about and yelp and wag before the grate empty of warmth. The china dogs had a wily look to their faces if you looked harder. The painted freckles on their flat muzzles were just like those of the Peke. Fluent painted lines feathered their china feet. Ailsa knew for a fact wally dugs were not the same as china bluetits. They were vernacular Scots ornaments, not substitutes for love.

Something quite warm and tender was about to take place in Ailsa's dream. She felt its approach like the opening of a door which has been ajar.

'Esme came in to it a new way, today,' said Carl, turning the pinky finger of his left hand around in the deep hairs of his left ear. He'd been feeling furred-up, slow, lately. 'I wasn't even angling for him yet, and up he leapt into the conversation. The old thing just looked me up and down after I'd eaten and said, "Esme Stewart was a lovely looking man, slim, with remarkably mannerly ways." How I had put her in mind of him I don't know, but I took it as a compliment.' He cleared his throat, pulled up his trousers by the belt which encircled the flesh below his belly, and rose to fetch another drink.

Catching on the silky loops of dog and baby at his feet, he tripped heavily, only saving himself by grabbing at the mantelpiece and keeping a hold on it to keep from falling on the two small creatures. Shocked, child and dog disentangled in one movement, like springs, and sat up alert, paired, huge-eyed, frozen by the hard tinkle of china all about them from the smashed wally dug whose widowed companion stared Ailsa hard in the eye as she felt the beautiful, romantic thing that had been approaching her recede.

'I'll get you another drink,' Ailsa said to Carl, angry enough to want to kill him.

THE WIFE AT NUMBER SEVEN
Christina Mills

Talk about surprise. His face hits the flerr an ah know ah've
landed him wan in the solar plexus. An tae be honest ye know
ah dae feel that wee bit guilty, for he's had no much ae a life,
what with his Da an aw lost at sea an his mother left tae rear
him an his brothers up. Terrible when ye think, but ye can
take sympathy so far, for see if it hadn't been for that woman
Devlin ah met in Duke Street, ah'd be none the wiser yet, for
seemingly everybody bar me knows. Ah mean ah knew, jist
knew, something was up. For like he wears noo a tie, something he used tae never, an he's dropped years since he's lost
his beer belly; an much as it chokes me tae say, never has he
looked better, but by Jove, does he no owe me an explanation,
for see when she turnt round an telt me that? Well. Imagine.
Ah couldnae wait fast enough tae get up the stair, an see when
ah did, it's sitting like Lord Muck waiting the dinner getting
ready; an so ah goes, 'Explain yourself you right big sod ye!
Imagine. After aw ma years tae. Are ye worth it? Like hell ye
are! Well, let me tell ye something you, you're a real star turn
you. You know that? Ma da was right aw these years ago, for
see as a man, you leave a lot tae be desired. So ye dae.'

If looks could kill, ah'd be deid. Ah mean, it's no as though
he's bad at heart really, for he's no but. No when ye hear
about others an the kind ae things they get up tae. For he
dotes on the weans. Fair dotes. Reads them tae bed nights.
Aye. Jist as well for him he's got some redeeming features.
Aye.

He swallowed before opening his mooth. 'For the life ae me
ah don't know what you're prattling on about. Don't. If ah
did ah might be able tae help. Might. But you know your
trouble, don't ye, you listen tae too much gossip. Well then,
carry on, who's stopping ye. No me ah'm sure.'

Noo who's left feeling lousy, for it's no so long ago since his mother was got at the back ae the door, deid. May it was, for ah maself took the phone call that morning fae Benny his brother, an he went, 'That you Leezie? You no seen ma maw? She's no been seen at the shops. Neither our crowd nor Tommy's seen her. Any idea she could be? Think something's up? Ah think so. Think ye could pass a message tae our Ron tae get up the hoose pronto, see how things are doing? Cheers.'

Oh then ah felt for ma man. More so when he gret how he broke the door in; an picked her up and put her on the bed, an there she lay. Imagine. Five sons an no a wan near her. But fine wan me tae talk; for neither did ah go see her much, so felt bad ah did, an ah gret as much for maself as for him, an ah bought half a dozen ae these gladioli. Laid them tap ae her box, ah did, an aw her far flung relatives crowded in ben the room. saying things like: 'Cannae really complain, she's had a good innings. Many a slap round the ear hole she dished out in her day. Oh aye,' then after got mucked intae steak pie, sandwiches, an gab-gabbed an downed the whisky. But me, ah felt bad, felt outae it. Like noo.

ben

So turning ma back ah said no another word, an as soon as ah could ah got the dinner by, an packing the weans tae bed watched telly a bit, then made maself for bed with him at ma back falling over his big feet tae get there tae, an as soon as we were in bed he started his nonsense up an so ah goes: 'Excuse me, dae ye mind?' an bunged back his hand from off ma chest. Unbelievable. Must think me daft or something, but still, he got the message an laid off. Honestly, that desperate ah was tae get married that ah never thought about his job, the muck, the smell, the grease an the sight ae his nails. Black. An the swarfega he uses, well, still disnae really shift it. Anyway, see by the time the morning came was ah no glad tae see the back ae him, for ye had tae be there yourself tae hear the way he shouted the weans for the least wee thing; for no putting the cap back on the toothpaste, for leaving the bathroom a mess. Imagine. Him. For he could well have been describing himself, an so ah goes: 'Shut you your face up. Fine wan you tae talk,' an so with a face like fizz he slapped bang out the door. Much it bothered me. For aw ah cared he could go hang.

Ah then began the tidying up, an jist as ah was getting intae the swing ae things the phone went an this voice goes: 'Hullo. Hope you don't mind me phoning but this's Elizabeth Stuart, Liz for short. I'm a friend, that is of Ron's. I'd like to come talk to you about something. May I, if it's not too cheeky asking?'

Well, jist imagine how ah felt, anyhow, ah'll no elaborate, for ah jist cut right in with, 'Sunday suit ye? Say wan o'clock make it, OK?' an banged the phone down. Well, ah like that. Some people. No backward at coming forward. Really. Unbelievable. It really is.

But see the more ah thought about it the more worse ah got an the more worse ah got the more ah got worked up about it, tae something inside me snapped; an the next thing ah knew ah started tearing strips from off the wall: huge big chunks ae wallpaper. Dauds an dauds ae it, plaster an aw, tae ah was near deid on ma feet an fit for nothing by the time he came in that night. An as for him, well, he jist took wan look an said something like: 'Aw no, tell me ah'm dreaming,' an stood looking round. 'What's aw this in aid ae anyway? An another thing, how we supposed tae eat dinner with aw this guddle about?', that ah jist laughed an ah goes, 'What dinner ye talking about?' An ah jist about went intae hysterics at the look on his face. For it was tremendous, brilliant even.

Sunday then for me couldnae come fast enough. Like he was getting ma nerves, spouting things like: 'If ah'm the rank badgin you maintain ah am, how come you still here? You explain that? The door's open you know. You're free tae any-time go. Much you love me seeing as how you turn your back the minute ye get in bed. How you think that makes me feel? You that's supposed tae be a mother. Supposed tae understand. How d'you like out your bed five in the morning delivering milk, hitching papers around, aw before school starts an being late for it; an being strapped for good measure. Thank God ma sons'll never know the likes ae that. That's how if ah've tae diddle every posh twit that brings me his car intae the garage for this, that, an the next thing, ah'll dae it. Ah'll get ma ain back. You see if ah don't.' Then gret, then asked me tae forgive him, that he didnae mean what he said.

'You know me,' he said, but ah was beginning tae wonder.

Same tae the boys. 'What's ma daddy getting angry for?' Colin, ma eldest, went. Funny, ye never think they listen, but they dae so, an ah'd tae hush him up, an promise he and his wee pals could come up sometime an play with his train set. 'Promise mammy?'

'Cross ma heart an hope tae die.' An away he an wee Alec, taking Jim's hand went tae school. Ye could see they were dead chuffed; whilst me, ah stood at the window ages, waving like anything mad as they disappeared round by the Parade. Then see after for some reason ah started tae greet an could ah stop, ah couldnae. Ah gret. Ah laughed. Then gret again, an that's no me. No unless it's aw this worry an the fact that this woman's coming, or lassie whatever. Oh yes aye.

Sunday when it came broke nice an mild an ah nipped in ma slippers down tae Bob's for the *Sunday Post*. Great isn't it how August brings the rain an the worms that lie squidged in a figure eight on the pavement under your very feet; an the kind ae funny smell; the same kind ae smell that came from his mother when she lay togged up in her box, deid. Aye. For see how Sunday was here, ah wish noo it wasnae. For ah felt sick. Sick tae ma stomach. But as it was, the morning fair flew in, an ah took him his breakfast through, for ah figured the sooner that by, the quicker he'd be up an intae the papering, for honestly the place's a mess, so dumping him with his tray ah left an went through tae the weans' room; an they grabbed me, 'Play ghosties mammy,' an so getting a sheet ah put it tap ma head an went 'whoo-ooo-ooo.' An did they no squeal. They no half did. An dive-bombed under the bed clothes, an wee Jim, well, he near wet himself, for he was the last under. But see me, ah was a bag ae nerves, an kept going the toilet. Ah thought ah would never stop.

An so see when the door did go an ah opened it, there these wee chaps were an wan ae them goes: 'Colin says we can come up see his train. He says you say it's OK. He in?' an jist at that Colin came through, 'Can they mammy? Can they?' So ah goes, 'Aye, okay then. But mind no make it long noo,' an in they came. They no sooner disappeared ben the room when the door went; an it was her, an could ah take ma eyes off. Ah couldnae. Ah mean, who in their right mind comes tae anybody's door, dressed like that.

As it was, ah was tight-lipped as anything.

'Oh hullo. Come in. It's this way through here.'

She followed me ben through tae the kitchen, an see when he gets a load ae us two coming in, he jist about did his nut. He seemed tae swallow a glass ae water too fast for his ain good, an like he goes; 'Oh hear the weans, they're wanting me for something,' then scarpered out past us an slap banged the door shut.

Ah looked at her. She looked at me back.

Imagine. Ma lord an master an he couldnae even stand his ain ground. Ah was that embarrassed. Ah mean there's me, married against aw opposition, took aw the stick going, aw because that night ah stood talking him outside the Odeon in Renfield Street waiting a bus taking us home, an his eyes never left me, an ah fell for him an he saw me home tae ma place, an kissed me in the close where the wee inshot was.

An noo look this mess. It's well seeing he cannae see beyond the length ae his ain nose; talking ae which, ah'm right convinced a snotter stuck it as he scooted by.

She on the other hand tittered. 'Oh dear. *Mea culpa.* Afraid he obviously had no idea I was on my way up. I somehow had the idea you would say. Let him know. No wonder it came as a bit of a shock.' She shook her head. 'Poor dear. Still, I'm sure he'll survive.' She looked round for a place tae sit then planked herself on a chair; an it was as much as ah could dae tae haud the sink for support, as church bells ding-donged in Whitehill Street an ah felt the same as when that scunner ae a teacher rammed home the fact ae ma round shoulders an stuck me with her pole like a miniature Jesus out in front ae the class, saying, 'You poor?' An ah jist said aye, jist tae agree with her but ah felt sick. Like noo.

*

'You decorating?'

'Noo what person sits clacking gum in people's faces.'

'You surprised me phoning?'

'No the least, no really. Except, what really brings you here? See me was it?'

She shook her head no. 'Who knows. He not tell you by the way the accident we had? Last week. Sunday to be exact. We were out for a run. Brakes jammed. It was my birthday you understand. But it was just one of those things that happened. Could have happened anywhere. We were on our way to Balmaha . . .'

'Accident? Accident? What accident? First ah've heard ae it.'

'He didn't? Goodness, I've gone and put my foot in it, haven't I?' She sniggered. 'We ended up you know sitting drinking tea in a graveyard of all things. Actually people from nearby in some houses gave us it. But boy, did I suffer, did we suffer I should say. How's Ron been by the way? I got away with a few bruises, nothing very much. I think he was in much the same shape himself. You sure he didn't say?'

Well, is this no a fine how d'ye do. For who gives a rap about her birthday. But fancy him. Him. For him it was that took me for ma birthday the same place, tae a field we parked the side ae, an there three horses glued tae the skyline, stood on a hill. Ah remember down tae the last detail everything. The bees, the zizzen, the grass, the cows amalgamated thegether, the black map ae Africa on the side ae wan. We spread the mat. Broke the champagne open. Drank. Ate strawberries. Chucked the stalks away. Then he lashed out with more in ma glass an ah near swallowed, stalks an aw. An we laughed. Joked. We kissed. Got engaged. An noo look. This.

Is it any wonder you get the heart taken out ye, an so ah goes, 'You best go. No point you staying. This really disnae involve you. It's me an him for it, so if ye don't mind.' Ah went tae make as if for the door, but she got her neb in quick.

'Oh I don't agree. Don't. I mean I knew there could be the chance of things not working out right, that it could be counter-productive; but as it was, it was a risk worth taking.' She smiled, 'It's my life too you know.'

Well, ah tried tae no let the anger get the better ae me, for ma quarrel is with him, no her. For so help me, ah cannae even begin tae take her serious.

'As ah say, you best vamoose. Surely boyfriends at your age is no a problem is it?'

That needled her it did.

'Oh now I get the connection. I'm getting the hands off this is a married man routine, but dare I say, who are you to tell me what to do? How I should behave? You think I asked for this to happen? Not by a long chalk. But it did. So there, end of discussion. But at least I thought we could be adult about this, a let reason prevail kind of thing, but it was too much to ask. It always invariably is.'

Well. The nerve ae the wee thing, an jist as ah'm away tae dae ma pieces, in he comes, an as if it's the most natural thing in the world goes, 'Hi there! Sorry ah had tae dash like that but ye know what kids are, the wee menaces,' an drawing up a chair aside her, sat calm, composed, like Whistler's *Mother*.

She leaned a bit towards him: 'I was worried, not knowing how you were, for I don't know how you felt, but I felt like a wet rag afterwards, I don't mind telling you.' She touched him. 'You sure you're OK? You wouldn't lie to me or anything like that, would you?' She leaned even closer.

An damn me if he no laughed.

'Don't be a wee silly.'

See when ma voice came it felt somewhat funny. It addressed him.

'Ah don't know what you think you're playing at, but whatever it is ye better wind it up fast. Real fast.'

'Me?'

'Aye. You.'

She was jist away tae say something, but ah shut her up quick. 'Jist go an don't bother me you.'

She looked as if she couldnae believe her ears. He looked mad.

'Look. Try an listen. Ah'm trying tae be reasonable, tae be a gentleman . . .'

'A gentleman? You? Don't make me laugh. You're the

colour ae being a gentleman. You widnae know how. You know what your mother said? She said, "Ah got quality second time around." You know, ah know, Benny was her everything, her all. Her reason for living. You were Mr Nobody. For you she had tae marry. You ruined her life. Her chances. So don't you talk. Ever.'

She mumped something. He went white

'Right,' he shouted. 'Enough said. Remember who you're talking tae, an if it comes tae it, remember your manners. It's no too much tae ask ae ye surely.'

Well, ah don't believe in God. Ah don't go tae church, but ah dae believe in something, what ah don't know, so try ah dae no tae be foul mouthed. What good's it dae, but see noo?

'You swine. You absolute swine. Well seeing you don't see yourself as ah see ye, if ye did the truth would daunt ye. A grown man feart ae the dark, feart he hears a door opening, feart his mother'll come an staun an watch him, though what for ah don't know. She knew him for the toady he is. Toady. Toadies tae anything. Tae aul Nick himself if he thought it would get him anything.'

Oh the look on his face.

'Look understand something you . . .'

Noo see when anybody takes that tone ae voice with me, it usually means wan thing. Trouble.

A FAMILY DISGRACE
Deborah Moffatt

My sister Sylvia disappeared in the summer of 1976. At the time, we assumed that she had eloped with her boyfriend, Oscar Barrientos. It was a great disgrace and a terrible shock for my parents. My father, who held himself responsible for Sylvia's virtue and our family's honour, felt the disgrace most deeply, while my mother was less ashamed but more distraught at having lost her daughter. As Sylvia's brother, I was supposed to feel some sort of responsibility for her, just as my father did; in our society, the men in a family are expected to protect their women's virtue. But I was only a teenager at the time, and I wasn't really concerned with, or even fully aware of such things as family honour or women's virtue.

We assumed that Oscar and Sylvia had eloped, even though there was no real reason for them to do so. That they were in love had never been a secret. Neither family had objected to their relationship. Marriage had not been discussed, but it would almost certainly have been permitted. Nevertheless, when the couple disappeared, we all immediately thought that they had eloped because, at that time, we simply couldn't imagine any other possible reason for their disappearance.

Until then, my family had been quite friendly with the Barrientos. There had always been plenty of coming and going between our two houses – theirs a large two-storey villa in the old part of town, with a high wall hiding the house from the street and a spacious garden to the back, and ours a cramped apartment in a government housing estate on the far edge of town. Mostly the comings and goings had been to and from the Barrientos house, with far fewer visits from the Barrientos to us. We were often invited to their house for long Sunday afternoon *asados*, where there was always plenty to eat, more than enough to drink, and a steady stream of conversation.

My parents usually did most of the talking, and invariably they talked about politics, and always, when talking about politics, they argued.

My father was a staunch Peronist. He had a habit of saying, 'Perón made me what I am,' by which he meant to praise Perón. My father was a bricklayer by trade, but when he was still a young man he had started his own construction company, the first of many, all of which ended in bankruptcy. Despite his repeated failures, he saw himself as a success, a man of power and wealth, a self-made man. '*Soy patrón!*' he liked to say. 'If not for Perón, I would still be a poor bricklayer, working like a black for someone else!'

My mother had no praise for Perón. She was a Communist, a Party member. She had worked in the textile factories as a young girl, and always referred to herself as a worker, which irked my father, who insisted that our family was *not* working-class! He often said that he would never allow his wife to work, but of course she did work, not in the factories but at home, as a dress-maker, creating elegant suits and fine gowns for the wealthy women of our town. My father tried to pretend that she sewed for her own amusement rather than for the money she earned, but the truth was that we might have starved if my mother had not been such a hard worker and a skilled seamstress.

Both my mother and my father were strong-willed, very stubborn, never likely to concede a point in any argument. When they discussed politics, they would yell and scream at one another, trading insults and even obscenities freely, scarcely bothering to listen to what the other had to say. Their arguments were always loud and raucous and rude, no matter where they were; even at the Barrientos's home they carried on like wild animals, screeching and roaring and pounding the table so hard that the jug of wine would jump and the glasses would topple over.

Dr Barrientos rarely got involved in their arguments. He would push his chair away from the table, throw his head back, and watch my parents through half-closed eyes, his lips set in a slight, knowing smile. If he did speak, his voice would be soft, his tone conciliatory.

On our way homeward, my parents would ridicule the doctor. 'Who does he think he is?' my father would ask. 'He talks about Perón, but he has no idea what Perón meant to a man like me!'

'He is bourgeois,' my mother would state. 'Life has always been easy for him. He knows nothing of hard work, of suffering.'

Sylvia would defend the doctor. 'But Mamí – he does work hard! His surgery is open at all hours, and he is often at the hospital through the night, without –'

'And your father and I – look at how hard we work!' my mother would interrupt. 'But for all the work we do, we have no big house, no garden, no steak for *asados*! We will never have all that; not even Perón could give us such things,' she would conclude, intentionally goading my father into yet another argument.

He couldn't stand to be reminded of all the things we didn't have. We were poor, but we weren't supposed to admit it, not even to ourselves. We disguised our poverty well. Like most of the other families in town, we belonged to the country club, went on summer holidays to the beach, dressed ourselves in expensive clothes with well-known labels – Lacoste, Adidas, Levis. In order to pay for the clothes and the holidays and the club membership, we had to make little economies here and there. We spent very little on food, and sometimes, when my father's business wasn't doing well, we went hungry. We lived in a tiny, bare apartment. Sylvia shared a bedroom with my parents; I slept on the living-room sofa. In summer, the small apartment was unbearably hot and rank with the smell of sweat and rotting vegetables. In winter, if there was no money to buy paraffin for heating fuel, we huddled together around the kitchen table, warming ourselves over plates of thin broth.

Dr Barrientos often told me how lucky I was. 'I envy you, Carlitos,' he would say. 'To be a young man in Argentina today – what a life you have ahead of you! This is a land of opportunity, take my word for it!' He advised me to forget about politics. 'Don't bother with Marx; pay no attention to Perón. Read literature – Goethe, Proust, Shakespeare. You will find everything you need to know about life in literature, not in political pamphlets! Study the arts; read books; play music.'

I did as he suggested. I learned to play the guitar and spent hours practising scales and chords. My parents warned me that I was wasting my time. 'You'll never amount to anything if you sit around playing the guitar all day,' my father said. My mother was more direct. 'Go out and learn a trade,' she said. 'You'll starve to death if you don't.'

But Dr Barrientos said, 'Play music! For God's sake, if there is music in your soul, then you must let it out!'

He wasn't entirely happy with the music I played. 'Those folk tunes, and the tangos – well, they are very nice, I suppose, but they're dull, uninspiring. You must listen to jazz! Jazz is magnificent. It is – I don't know!' He waved his hands in the air in graceful, slightly flamboyant circles, searching for a way to express himself. 'I really don't know how to describe it. Jazz is transcendent; do you know what I mean?'

He took me into the living room, sat me down before an expensive stereo, and handed me a glass of whisky. 'You can't appreciate jazz when you're sober,' he explained. 'Drink.'

He played his records for me: Django Reinhardt, Oscar Alemán, Stan Getz, Miles Davis. Most of the music was old, had been recorded in the fifties or even earlier, but to me it was new, almost frighteningly modern.

Dr Barrientos poured out more whisky. 'You'll like it when you understand it,' he assured me. He played the records over and over, pointing out all the subtleties, the nuances of shading, of phrasing, of pitch, the inspired improvisations, the complexities of the rhythms and the harmonies. Just before a favourite passage, he would put up a finger, whisper, 'Listen!' and then lean back, with his eyes closed. 'Aaaah!' he would sigh. 'Did you hear that, Carlitos, eh?'

During the winter, when Oscar and Sylvia were away at university, I visited the doctor almost every day. My father disapproved. 'You should be studying, or working, instead of wasting your time with that music,' he would say. 'Jazz! What sort of nonsense is that? What's wrong with the tango? With Gardel?'

When Oscar and Sylvia came home that summer, the doctor had no time for me. I was still welcome to come to his house, of course, and I was allowed to listen to his records, but he didn't listen to them with me, because he was too busy listening to Oscar and Sylvia and all their talk. They had discovered politics at university, and that was what they talked about, to anyone who would listen.

My father refused to hear a word. 'You children know nothing! Guerrilla wars, underground armies? Mahhh! Make-believe! There was no such foolishness when Perón was alive!'

My mother wouldn't listen to them either. 'Study Marx,' she said. 'Join the Party. Then we'll talk about revolution.'

I didn't listen to them. Political talk always sounded the same to me: Oscar and Sylvia, my mother, my father, all seemed to be saying the same thing. They believed that they had the answers to life's problems, but Dr Barrientos, with his superior smile and soft tones, hinted that nobody really had any answers at all.

I tried hard to regain the doctor's attention. I played his favourite records, turning up the volume little by little to be sure that he heard. He scolded me: 'I know that in your family you like a lot of noise, but here we are different.' Blushing, I turned the volume to its lowest setting.

I learned to play one of Oscar Alemán's numbers, and proudly performed it for the doctor. 'But you've missed the whole point!' he exclaimed. 'You're just imitating someone; that isn't jazz! You must learn to improvise, to play the tune in your own way.'

I bought a record by a Brazilian jazz musician whose name was new to me. I hoped to impress the doctor with my discovery. He glanced at the record sleeve and said, 'Never heard of him. Play it, if you like.' Then he turned his attention back to Oscar and Sylvia.

The music broke into the room, an anguished cry from a rasping saxophone.

'Stop that hideous noise!' Dr Barrientos cried. 'Do you really mean to tell me that you like that? My God, haven't I taught you *anything* about music?'

I lifted the needle with a shaking hand, scratching the record.

'Carlitos!' The doctor's voice was thin with exasperation. 'Please, be careful!'

'Papi, listen,' Oscar begged. 'We're trying to tell you something!'

'And I am *trying* to listen!' Dr Barrientos snapped. 'Really, children, can't you all just calm down?' He rubbed his temples with his fingertips. 'Settle down, enjoy life, please! You're all trying to grow up so fast. You think you know everything there is to know, already – you two, Oscar and Sylvia, with your politics, and Carlitos with his music – but you've only just begun to learn. Take your time, take life as it comes. Enjoy yourselves while you're young!'

'But how can we?' Sylvia asked. 'Don't you see what's happening, here in this country? We must act now, or it will be too late!'

'Sylvia – be quiet!' Dr Barrientos' voice was polite, but stern. His smile was forced, brittle. 'I tell you, my child, you know nothing! If you had any idea, any idea at all, about life – about the past, about the hard times we've been through, your parents and I, you would understand just how lucky you are to be living here now, in this country, in these times. Just look at us – so happy, so well-fed, a roof over our heads! Here we are enjoying ourselves, drinking wine, talking freely about politics, without any fear at all – Sylvia, don't you see? This is the good life! And you want to change it? No, no; forget all this nonsense about politics. Enjoy yourselves, enjoy your youth while you can.' He sighed, and his smile relaxed. He leaned back in his chair. 'The good life, indeed. Drink! More wine, anyone? Carlitos – take off that awful record, and put on something we can all enjoy. Django, I think; eh?'

A month later, when we were on holiday at the beach, Oscar and Sylvia disappeared. They went out to a discotheque one night and never came back. It was assumed that they had eloped.

My father, in a fury, forbade me to have anything more to do with the Barrientos family. 'They have disgraced us! If I had only known what sort of people they were, I would never have allowed you to associate with them.'

He blamed Oscar for leading Sylvia astray. He blamed the doctor for raising a son who would do such a thing. He blamed himself – and me – for not protecting Sylvia. He felt the disgrace greatly.

A few years later, the Barrientos moved away. We heard that they were going to Spain. Most of the wealthy families in town were emigrating. Argentina was no longer a land of opportunity. Inflation was soaring; our money was good for nothing. We couldn't afford holidays at the beach or membership at the country club. There were no more lazy Sunday afternoon *asados*. Our clothes, Lacoste and Adidas and Levis, were worn through, patched and repatched. There was very little food on the table.

We began to hear whispered stories about the thousands and thousands of people who had disappeared without trace. There was talk of crowded prisons, of torture, of executions, mass burials. It was mostly hearsay; there was very little evidence, no proof. It was still possible to dismiss all such stories as lies, or exaggerations. It took us a long time to understand that what had appeared to be a family disgrace was, in fact, a national tragedy.

BEARSDEN BAGATELLE
William Oliphant

PART ONE
Fuhll Bladders in the Paurley

The news story transportit me back owr fifty year tae Parliamentary Road it the end i the twinties: 'The Paurley' i ma furst decade.

The Paurley runs (ur ran) fae Castle Street tae Sauchiehall Street which, although east n west, tae us wis aywis up n doon. The rid tramcaurs gaun up wur headit fur Bishopbriggs ur Millerston, the blue fur Alexandra Park. Oan the doon line, the rid wur fur Merrylee, Giffnock n Rouken Glen, n the blue, Kirklee ur Scotstoun. Thae names fae the destination boards wur aw familiar tae us long afore we iver saw thum is places, ur even knew whoar they wur.

The caurs thursels, sweein, clangin, thundern past oor coarner, wur essential features i the lanscape. It wis jist is if they hid occurred in Nature tae fillfu' the uses we pit thum tae. They produced the coloured doackets we collectit is substitutes fur cigarette cairds, they oaffered free hurls atween stoaps if ye wur brave enough tae hing oanty the brass haun-rail whin the conductor wis up the sterrs, n they wur a source a pleesure n terror if ye hud tae jump aff it speed. Aw kindsa explosive compounds wur detonatit bi thur iron wheels, beer boatle taps wur flattened bi thum, n the steel rails they ran oan wur convenient geometrical divisions in the roadway fur competitive purposes.

The gemme ah huv in mind hud nae pipe-baun waarm-up lik a Hampden afferr, bit it startit oaf wi a helluva loata runnin in in oota hooses fur drinks a watter. Minny a maw musta bin hert-roastit long afore the skaillin fuhllness a bladder, a precondition a entry, wis achieved.

Ah'm no talkin aboot kids jist peein in the street, even peein well oot intae the street. Kirbside urination hud bin elevatit tae the level a high art. We'd perfectit a technique thit involved fuhllin the space atween phallus n foreskin tae the latter swelt lik a fitba bladder, then releasin the pressure a finger n thumb so thit an atomized spurt hurtled itsel ootwards acroass the road. Wi due attention peyed tae trajectory n wind velocity phenomenal ranges wur achieved. We could aw reach beyond the saicant caur rail, n Wattie Houston, hauder i the championship, hud, wi a wee bit help fae a foaleyin wind thit swirled doon Black Street it the psychological moment, passed the thurd.

In the very nature a things we contendit is individuals, the wans thit did contend, that is. Francis Nimmo, ah mind, wis a non-starter because id bin circumcised is a wean. It wisnae the kinna gemme thit separatit us intae teams, cock ur hen, spit ur dry. No lik fitba wherr we identified wi Rangers or Celtic dependin oan whether we went tae Kennedy Street School ur St Mungo Primary. It the kirb each man stuck oot oan is ain, n although the spectators wur partisan, they wurnae sectarian.

Alastair Finn, wee hard man i the group a unemployed youths thit hung aboot the coarner, made a book whiniver we competit. He could calculate odds wi a facility thit nane i the Maths teachers in St Mungo's hud iver suspected, n bets wur laid, won n loast in hauf Woodbines. Excitement oaften ran high. Bladders wur fuhlled n empied, fuhlled again n empied, n oan a number i occasions weemin staunin oan the platforms a eastbound caurs hud thur stoackins sprayed bi mistimed ur over-enthusiastic ejections.

Ah suppose the Polis wid ultimately huv pit a stoap tae wur innocent fun – that's whut Polis wur fur in thae days – bit McTaggart beat thum tae it. McTaggart wis a bit bigger n aulder thin the rest i us. He wis kinna new tae the district, so nane i us kent much aboot um, n he hudny much tae say fur issel. Whin we lined the kirbside n committit wursels tae the excitement i the match, he usually stood tae the wan side n looked inscrutably oan.

Only wance did he cheynge this pattern. It wis durin a lull in the proceedins, while we restit n refuelled, he wis seen tae step tae the pavement's edge, unbutton is fly, n send an unbroken yellow stream in a great parabolic curve oot n beyond the fourth rail. Tae this day ah cin see the scunner oan Wattie Houston's face as he watched is hard-won record sae nonchalantly shattered.

We niver played the gemme again. McTaggart, it turned oot, wis ninety per cent foreskin. Ye canny compete wi deformity.

It wis in a copy i the *Westerton n Bearsden Chronicle* ah picked up accidentally thit ah saw the news story:

A sixty-five-year-old company director from Bearsden was fined £10 when he appeared at the Burgh Court on Monday. Walter Templeton Houston admitted charges of breach of the peace and indecent exposure outside his luxury flat in Grove Park. The Burgh Prosecutor told the Court that two nights earlier a police constable on patrol had seen the accused urinating from a fourth floor balcony. Houston was arrested and charged at Bearsden Police Station. Houston's agent said, 'My client is normally a moderate man, but he had taken drink that evening, and did not know what he was doing. He is extremely sorry and wishes to assure the Court that such an incident will not reoccur.' Earlier the Prosecution told the Court that Houston was heard to shout, 'How's that for the car rails?'

Ah read it through twice. It jist hud tae be the same Wattie Houston. Company director? Luxury flat? Wattie hud done well fur issel. Ah wunnered who ur whut hud driven um tae flaunt is origins oan is luxury balcony, whut conflict hud caused um tae regress aw the wey back tae the thurd caur rail oan Paurley Road. It wid've bin ridiculous fur me tae phone um – he wis jist a face na foreskin fae the mists i ma childhood (and a) – bit in ma imagination ah wis diallin is number.

'Mr Houston? As representative of the Paurley Pissers of the Past Association, ah regret tae hufty inform you thit yur recent record attempt his bin declerred null n void because a the advantage a elevation . . .'

Regression cin be infectious. That night in the bathroom, whin ah wis gettin ready fur ma bed, ah hud a sudden impulse tae try ma haun it the auld gemme. Mibby it wis lack a practice, mibby even sheer physical development, thit explains my disastrous failure. Is ah mopped up the lavvy flerr, ah reflected philosophically oan how minny things git loast in the years atween.

PART TWO
Visiting Marian

Easy, Wattie, easy. Gently now. There's a definite tendency to stagger and a definite tendency to spray on the labial plosives – oh God bless the labial plosives! – and a definite tendency to weep whisky tears into the beer, only there's no beer here.

Steady, Wattie. There's a pillar on the porch to lean against – Corporation Corinthian! – and a green door set in the faced brick – Council-House-Baronial! – and a cute little perspex rectangle with the name in black letters on silver paper: 'M. MCGONAGLE'. A mick! Slum Irish and Fenian. What the hell's she doing tied to one of those? There's a chromium bell push and the nipped sound of strangled chimes, plink-plonk like a double hernia, and Marian at the door, fat, dark, smiling and ready, and the smile fading a little when her notice is arrested by the sound and the stagger and the smell of the whisky.

Humble apologies to dear, sweet, accommodating Marian. She has seen you that way and yon, up and down, bird's eye and worm's eye, but never cut, never the need, and never now if it wasn't for the court this morning and that whining bastard of a lawyer and the indecent exposure. And how is she? And the six steps and stairs McGonagles that have all come out of her, and the big horny McGonagle who gives her babies and Christ knows what pleasures, except that they're not enough since she'll take all you can give her for pure enjoyment. And it's not lost what a friend gets. And a change is as good as a rest. And what nobody knows doesn't do them any harm.

Humble apologies to mollify Marian and the smile is back,
though the withdrawn look in the eye is the Saturday-night
calculation of dates. Don't wave your menstrual calendar at
me, Marian. That's for drunken Irish micks. This is me,
Wattie, cock with a Protestant conscience, user of contracep-
tive devices on every conceivable occasion, purveyor of many
pleasures and never an anxious moment despite your manifest predilection for pregnancy. And how's that for labial
plosives?

Now straight for the fire, Wattie, for it's raining misery
outside, and sit at the right hand with Marian opposite so you
can look up her skirt. Drink tea, the thick tarry brew which
seems always to be on the gas, and eat a roll, two rolls, with
spam. And talk! Talk the kind of talk you would never talk
sober. You can tell her she is beautiful and she will never
believe you mean it because of the whisky. Although in a way
it's perfectly true. Dear good old Marian with her belly
muscles slackening and her great breasts beginning to sag,
with the smur of blue hair under her oxters, the massive rotun-
dity of hips and the shaggy ridge of pelvis. Dear, fat, sweet
Marian, the only woman you know whose nakedness doesn't
proclaim, 'This is my body!' but quietly, 'This is me!' Self-
acceptance, and it makes her acceptable, and beautiful.

More tea, Wattie. More of the hot, sweet, tarry scald. Tea
is an aphrodisiac! Who needs it with the view up her skirt and
the way the weight of the teapot flexes her bare arm and
modifies the line of her breast? Hot and sweet, feed it to the
patient for shock.

Admit to the shock, Wattie. Admit to the shock of appearing
in that place for that reason, for all the arrogant air, for all
the sophisticated nonchalance. The man-about-town caught
short in public. And the bland, blond advocate full of the
confident courage of his own lies, and the world-bleary, idiot-
chinned naive sadist on the bench, and the smell of terror
from the drunk drivers waiting on the back row, and the smirk
and the sniff and the pencil-chewing Pitmans of the *Westerton
and Bearsden Chronicle*.

Admit to the shock, Wattie, and to the sudden up-rearing
vision of Agnes prostrate, mortally mortified, riding her sofa

in a shipwreck of shame, a peaky motionless figure on an overstuffed raft adrift on a neutral, opinionless sea of wall-to-wall. And that's what you wanted, Wattie, at the time. But it was the drink, and you're not used to the drink, and here we are again.

No, don't move, Marian!

Her movements are too provocative, and you still have all those words first before you lose your senses in her provocative movements, all those words the whisky has smoked up into the top of your brain, and they'll take your skull off like a Cherokee in a hurry if you don't open your mouth and let the words rumble out on to the floor. Or on to somebody's lap, on to Marian's lap, because it is so voluminous. If you can bury your face in such a lap and forget your fever, you can bury your words in it and maybe turn their edge.

Words! Words! Words! There was a time, Wattie when you wouldn't have had the words, but you've read a book or two since then. Walter T. Houston, Company Director, has the words, a plethora of words. Words are instruments that torture images.

'Agnes!' you would say in a tender moment. 'You're still the best feel in Bearsden.' And that would stiffen her. Yet the words were not what you meant, and she would have known that had she been listening to you with her guts instead of her brain. Well of course you've felt your way around Bearsden. Middle class arses, and they're not all cold, not by a long chalk, but they're all so bloody neurotic. Sex doesn't so much function as break out like a rash. It's a disease, an abnormality. For a couple to lie down together and have a straightforward enjoyable shag is some kind of perversion. Animal instincts! As if there were any other kind.

And Wattie! You don't really understand what it's all about, do you? What is it with Agnes and her middle class cronies, the vested virgins of the west? Middle class is the wrong term. You use it just as a derogatory noise, a label of contempt remembered from childhood contact with dole queues, hunger marches, slogans chalked on tenement walls, and fried bread. Bourgeois is just as meaningless, although it has more of a growl to it.

What is it then? It's not class, and it's not politics, and it's not long noses nor the West-end affectations of voice and syntax. But it has something to do with wall-to-wall carpeting and drinks on the sideboard and the abstract over the mantel-piece. And it has something to do with Daddy's money, even though, for Christ sake, Daddy started life as a common bricky, and it has to do with 'A Liberal View of Sexual Morality' with as little actual nookie as her man will put up with, and maybe — you don't know — but just maybe there is some guilt in it. Maybe there is guilt for a morganatic marriage, guilt for the working class bun in the middle class oven, guilt for being Wattie's feel, the best in Bearsden, a two orgasm woman caught in the mixter-maxter tradition of the 'Liberal View' on the one hand, and strict Calvinistic continence on the other.

All right, Agnes, all right! None of that is fair. When we come down to it, it's all a matter of humiliation. Wattie humiliated – the majesty of the Law triumphant. Agnes humiliated – her shame sprayed from her luxury balcony into her luxury courtyard within sight and sound of her luxury friends. And the two humiliations have still to meet and be reconciled, and may the good Lord preserve us all.

So move over, Marian McGonagle, who was Marian MacLelland a hundred fecund years ago, and move over, Wattie, to bury your face in the plump mother-breasts that cushion all the shocks, and your hands on the white, warm thighs, and the gall slowly draining away. And she'll not let you sleep too long, Wattie, if you should sleep, for the steps and stairs McGonagles will all be in from school at four.

PART THREE
Agnes on Stockie Muir

What she felt around her here was the sky and the cleansing Stockie Muir wind. The tussocky grass was wet from the morning's rain, but her boots were proof against it, and she was well clad, and knew how to avoid the real bogs. It was clear and bright now and Queen's View was glorious.

She had not come for the glories of the view or, indeed, for the enfolding sky or the antiseptic wind. She came because Bearsden stifled her. There were too many familiar faces in and around the shops, the hush of the library deafened her, and the church was merely the church; a place for gossip and flower-arranging, for cups of tea and sympathetic friends who said they were sorry and enjoyed their own compassion.

She could have gone to the Burgh Court this morning and gloated. But she refrained. The games they play there are inappropriate and irrelevant. Already, in her made-up mind, she had assembled all the facts and decided that they too were irrelevant. She had not come to the muir to think. The thinking was done. She had come to square her shoulders, to straighten a spiritual stoop that had, she became aware, been developing for years.

Away to her left she saw the Whangie, that strange formation of rock, cliff and chasm so beloved by the nursery climbers of Glasgow. She half-remembered the legend connecting it to the Devil's hoofprint, one step taken between the Islands and Edinburgh, before his heel-swerve south to fields more fertile for his purposes. She smiled at the thought of Auld Nick taken short on Stockie Muir and turning his great, black, pointed pintle to lay down Loch Lomond and shake off the drips to form the reservoirs between here and Dumbarton.

There was no smell now of Satanic influence. She stood in a small wet wilderness and, surrounded by it, experienced a sense of liberation. She was liberated by the sky and the wind, by rock and bog, by a teasing glimpse of loch and the view of mountains to the north. She was freed by the thought of Old Horny so spectacularly relieving himself. She remained perfectly still for a long time and breathed in what she took to be the spirit of the Muir. Then, as she turned and began to retrace her steps towards the car park, she consciously shed the burden of the Little-Boy-Lost, and watched, with some astonishment at her own detachment, a fading vision of a last, petulant flash of phallic pride, and a pathetic yellow stream splashing inaptly into the front lawn.

A CHILD AT YULE
Willie Orr

The seamen held the white blades of their oars against their shoulders and, dipping the shafts into the weed, pushed their craft stern-first towards the open sea. A gull perched unperturbed on the high prow, disdainfully surveying the small group of men left on the island. As the seamen shipped their oars, the birlin glided into the ripples beyond the point. The halyards screamed in the sheaves as they raised the sail and the startled gull left its perch, soaring effortlessly across the sea. MacLaine followed its flight while it floated in the summer wind, motionless in the current like a leaf in a stream. At first he watched it with little interest but, when it turned suddenly and flew south towards the distant cliffs, its freedom to depart reminded him of his own predicament and the thongs round his wrists.

The sail of the birlin filled and pulled the bow to leeward and, as it sailed away, MacLaine glanced at the two men beside him on the shore. They were taller than he and more than twenty years younger. The one nearest to him had long, fair hair, flowing like combed lint round his shoulders, and full lips which would have been effeminate had they not been twisted in a sneer. The continual changes of expression in his small blue eyes hinted at a volatile and unpredictable nature. He seemed to be cleft with contradictions – physically powerful yet curiously fragile, gentle yet cruel, humorous but grim. Dressed like a prince in a saffron tunic, a coloured cloak with brilliant crimson hems and flamboyant wolf-skin boots, he had an air of distinction but his manner was too coarse to play the role successfully. One of the men in the boat, now far offshore, shouted and waved his sword, which flashed in the sunlight below the sail. The blond one laughed and raised his middle finger rudely in reply. MacLaine caught him

exchanging glances with his companion. There was an inti-
macy between them which he found faintly distasteful.

The other man was dark and lean like a spent stag, the
lingering passion of the rut in his eyes and the smell of it on
his breath. As he laughed with his comrade, MacLaine could
imagine him bellowing in the mist, foam flying from his jaws
as he herded his hinds and drove off his rivals. Just a beast,
MacLaine decided, driven by instinct. He watched the two
men carefully, trying to assess their personalities and detect
weaknesses which he might exploit. One day, after all, he
might have to kill them.

The dark one seemed to sense his scrutiny, for his expression
changed quickly from humour to hostility and he unsheathed
his knife, moving towards the prisoner. MacLaine stepped
back, raising his bound hands to defend himself. For a
moment they crouched in anticipation, coiled for the attack,
until the blond intervened, laughing at their tense hesi-
tation.

'He was going to cut you free, MacLaine,' he said, stepping
in front of his companion and gently removing the knife from
his trembling hand, 'Were you not, Domhnull?'

There was no answer.

'Besides, you are worth more alive,' he continued, cutting
through the thongs on MacLaine's wrists, 'Come, let us look
at our quarters.'

He set off along the shore, raising a flock of sea-pies from
the pebbles. Domhnull glanced aggressively at MacLaine and
followed, his bare feet scarcely marking the turf.

MacLaine watched them, the blond leaping easily from
stone to stone at the end of the beach and the dark one walking
awkwardly behind him. It was when the latter turned to look
back that MacLaine realized that he had seen him before. He
could not recall the circumstances but the image of the man
glancing back stirred a strange blend of emotions, ranging
from sorrow to intense anger. He tried to remember the
occasion but the more he concentrated the more the memory
faded and, when the man turned away, it vanished completely, leaving him frustrated and uneasy. He was sure that
Domhnull had experienced the same sensation, for, during

the voyage from Mull, he had caught him staring with a frown as if he too was trying to recall their previous encounter.

He massaged the weals on his wrists and flexed his fingers, noticing how the muscles moved on his forearm. He clenched his fist and admired the evidence of strength in his sword arm. He could still lift a cheese stone with that hand. But he could not swim and with that deficiency he was as effectively imprisoned on the island as a man half his size. He thought of his young wife and remembered her frail arms in the grip of the Irishmen. She had not cried when they burst into the room and pulled her roughly from the bed to hold her against the wall with a knife at her throat. He remembered her eyes in the flickering light of the pine torches pleading with him to contain his rage. Her dignity and calm had astonished him. As he thought of it, he longed to hold her again and touch her closed eyelids with his fingers. He wondered if the Irishmen employed by his kinsman to capture him had spared her and, if they had, whether he would ever see her again. His reflections were interrupted, however, by a shout from his blond gaoler, who was beckoning from a cleft in the rocks.

He considered making a protest by ignoring the signal but, on second thoughts, decided that it would be wiser to foster a sense of security in his guards so that, if an opportunity to escape arose, his swift reaction might surprise them. He followed them slowly, studying the island carefully.

It was virtually bisected from north to south by a high plateau flanked by parallel basalt precipices reaching almost from shore to shore. The centre of the island, therefore, formed an impregnable refuge and this natural protection had been reinforced with a curtain wall in places that might have provided access to the summit. About halfway along the eastern cliff there was a narrow gateway, through which he followed his guardians, climbing a stone stairway to the plateau. As they emerged, he was amazed at the abundance of the pasture and the array of wild flowers among the grass. There were two buildings in front of them, both constructed with black island stone and roofed with divots.

'This is our home, then,' the blond announced with little enthusiasm, 'at least till they come to take us back.'

'And you, MacLaine,' Domhnull added with obvious relish, 'may be here till you die.'

'A dismal thought, Domhnull – and him with a young wife too.'

MacLaine involuntarily reached for his knife, only to find an empty belt. He tried to conceal his mistake by adjusting the buckle but his reaction had not been missed and the pretence made him look foolish. He glared into the blue eyes only to be thrown by their gentleness. Expecting to find scorn or malice, he found compassion and this disturbed him. He was dealing with someone whom he could not understand and his failure to fathom his enemy worried him. Besides, the folds and fires of the man's hair reminded him of his wife. Indeed every time he looked at him from behind he was shocked by the resemblance.

'Be kind to our guest, Domhnull,' the young man said quietly. 'It will be a long winter.'

They entered the nearest building, stooping to avoid the low lintel. There was only one doorway, leading into a long, dark room with a smaller chamber at the south end.

'Your quarters, MacLaine,' the blond nodded towards the latter.

MacLaine entered and looked round the cell, assessing his chances of escape. They were very slim. The arrow-slit windows admitted little light and offered no hope of exit and the heavy, hewn door could be closed with a massive bar on the outside. It was pointless anyway, he remembered, to plan an escape from the building when he had no boat. He examined the rest of the room with little interest. In the corner a woollen mattress lay on a bank of heather roots and a single chair had been left behind the door. The crucks supporting the roof were damp and, even in midsummer, glistened with rust-coloured slime. He was relieved to see a fireplace in the wall and driftwood left by the last occupant, for he knew that the winter storms, which swept across the channel from Ireland, could last for weeks. The earth floor, which was dry and firm at that moment, would be damp and unpleasant in the winter.

*

He was allowed to wander everywhere on the plateau but was forbidden to descend to the shore unless accompanied by one of the guards. He found a place above the cliffs at the south end of the island, a seat among the rocks lined with sedge and thrift from which he could see the white sands of the holy island and watch the seaways for ships. Occasionally galleys passed but, seeing the banner flying above the fortifications, their captains never altered course to visit the island. As the terraced hills of Mull lost their summer grass and the bracken withered to cover the slopes with irregular patches of russet decay, MacLaine began to despair. He could see no way of building a boat or obtaining a bladder to carry him across to Mull. There were neither cattle nor sheep on the island, their only meat being the salt beef landed with them in the summer.

To vary their diet he used horsehair lines to catch saithe from the rocks and fashioned an eel from a strip of leather off his belt, binding it round the hook with silver wire from his brooch, and caught red lythe in the flood tide. With the cold weather, however, they had vanished from the shore.

The other building on the island was a chapel and MacLaine made a point of visiting it in the evening. It was empty apart from a carved stone cross and a battered pewter chalice which lay in a recess in the drystone wall but, when the door was shut, it seemed to possess a profound calm, a primeval tranquillity, which even the westerly gales could not disturb. MacLaine always knelt on the schist flags not because he was a particularly religious person but because he felt more at ease in that position.

When he tried to pray or recited the rosary, the Holy Mother always assumed the form of his wife with the hair of the blond warrior. At first the image enraged him and he fled from the chapel, beating his forehead with his hands to erase it, but gradually he became reconciled to the strange portrait and the diverse emotions which it stirred began to subside. The chapel became the place where he thought of his wife, a sanctuary in which he could release his misery and express his longing in prayers. He made a lamp with a rush wick and a cockle shell filled with fish oil so that he could remain in his refuge after dark. His guards did not seem to mind when he carried an ember from his fire across to the chapel.

One night, just after Martinmas, he woke suddenly. A strange silence lay over the island, almost palpable in its intensity. He stopped breathing and listened. There was no sound from the sea and even the seabirds were quiet. Rolling out of his cloak, he rose and listened again at the door. He was sure that his gaolers were not there. When he tried the latch, he discovered that the door was not barred and that the room seemed to be empty. Returning to the fire, he found a smouldering twig, blew it aflame and, holding it above his head, emerged from his cell. The beds were indeed empty and, beside one of them, lay a sword. He hurried over and, sliding it from its sheath, measured its weight in his hand, feeling its balance. It was shorter than his own two-handed weapon but evidently made by a master craftsman.

He opened the door slowly, expecting to see the guards but there was no one there. Outside, the full moon lit the island from the south, casting a long, glittering shaft of light on the sea. He noticed that there was also a faint light in the chapel and tried to reach the building quietly but the grass was crisp with frost and his bare feet crunched as he moved. Nevertheless he reached the shadow undetected and, keeping well back, peered through one of the windows. What he saw through the murky glass so astonished him that he swore audibly.

The two men were kneeling in front of the cross but they were not praying. As he watched, Domhnull, with extraordinary tenderness, passed his fingers through his companion's hair. MacLaine was mesmerized and completely confused. He had rarely seen such gentleness and affection but he had never seen it expressed by one man to another. He found it beautiful and repugnant, fascinating but horrifying. To add to the chaos of his emotions he could not detach his longing for his wife from the hair of the blond mercenary in the chapel. Suddenly he realized that he could not kill the man. He could not slice open the neck beneath his wife's hair. He turned away and furiously tossed the sword towards the sea. It hummed through the air, shimmering in the moonlight, and curved over the cliff to crash on the rocks below.

He returned to his quarters, rolled himself in his cloak again and forced himself to sleep, trying to remember where he had seen the dark one before. He understood why these men had been chosen as his guards and why their isolation was not a burden to them.

Just before Yule a storm broke over the island from the southwest. The thunder of the waves against the cliffs seemed to shake the sturdy building and the roof cabars bent and creaked with the force of the wind. Even the rocks hung on ropes over the roof to steady the divots began to roll against the walls. Rain streamed down the crucks and the floor, apart from a ring round the fire, turned black and soft. For four days the storm beat against the cliffs, saturating the atmosphere and every garment in the house with salt spray, and then, as quickly as it had arrived, it subsided.

MacLaine returned to his seat above the cliffs to enjoy the weak winter sun and watch the residual swell swirl round the rocks. His guards never mentioned the sword but they had carefully barred his door every night since their visit to the chapel. During the day, however, they allowed him to gather driftwood on the shore for the fires. In his presence they betrayed no sign of their illicit relationship, Domhnull, if anything, being more surly than before. As he gazed towards the south MacLaine remembered the scene in the chapel and was about to disentangle his own reactions to it when he noticed the gulls quarrelling over a large piece of flotsam below him.

He knelt on the edge of the cliff and tried to discern its shape. It was the carcass of a black cow. He could see its tail and horns beneath the surface. Long white ribbons of entrails spread out like tentacles from its gut, undulating gently in the tide. Suddenly he leapt to his feet and began to throw stones frantically at the gulls, trying to drive them away.

As the carcass drifted towards the shore he walked back towards the centre of the island, where there was access to the western creek, moving casually to avoid arousing suspicion. His gaolers were absorbed in the task of breaking firewood. Once out of their sight, he ran along the rocks, caught the carcass by the leg and pulled it through the water to the beach. It took all his strength to haul it above the high water mark and cover it with sods kicked from the bank. It was imperfectly concealed but he hoped that it would remain undiscovered till he could find a sharp implement to skin it and return the flayed carcass to the sea. He cursed his folly in discarding the sword. He searched for it but, as he expected, it had been carried away by the storm.

To his dismay the birlin returned the following day, landing in the western creek. The guards rushed down to the shore, passing so close to the carcass that he expected them to notice the heap of sods. Fortunately they were too eager to speak to the crew to see anything unusual. He watched them from the cliff until they called him down to help them unload the bags of meal and sides of salt beef.

As he approached the ship, a figure clothed in hodden grey was lifted over the gunwale and set upon the shore. It was an elderly woman, slightly stooped and shivering in the cold wind. The blond led her by the hand towards MacLaine.

'Your kinsman has sent you a companion,' he smiled. Behind him the crew laughed and shouted crude comments.

MacLaine was furious. His kinsman's gesture was unlikely to be an expression of compassion and therefore must be an insult. As he glanced at her sallow face, creased like a battle coat, and her calm, submissive eyes, he dismissed his own affront and considered her feelings. Her despatch to the island, whether motivated by benevolence or malice, may have injured his pride, but it showed an inexcusable contempt for the lady. Removing his cloak, he placed it round her shoulders and, glaring at the seamen, led her towards the plateau.

'Come, cailleach. Ignore them. They are coarse creatures, who sell themselves for silver.'

He led her to the chapel.

'You will live here,' he said with a hint of embarrassment as he realized that his refusal to share his quarters might add to her injuries. 'I will make a fire for you and see to your needs.'

'I was instructed to see to yours,' she replied with such

extraordinary dignity and frankness that he felt immediately
at ease with her.

'My only need is to escape from this place.'

He carried driftwood and water for her through that winter
and broke a hole in the thatch to let the smoke escape. He
brought her saithe and sea-parrots, which he caught with a
horsehair noose. Domhnull soon abandoned his coarse
remarks and Cathair, who had watched MacLaine's reaction
to the woman with some curiosity, eventually lost interest.
His companion, however, with infuriating regularity, asked
MacLaine if he would like to pray in the chapel before he
barred the door.

In the meantime MacLaine worked on his means of escape.
Using a piece of glass from the chapel window, he skinned the
cow, pushed the carcass out to sea and stretched the hide in
a crevice in the cliff face. He began to gather strips of wood
to form ribs for the currach and picked pitch from the pleats
of his battle coat to seal the seams. Yet the sea cast up few
pieces of timber which were suitable and he often despaired
of escaping from the island.

In those black days he would lie on his bed and think of
home, tormenting himself with fantasies and, when the skeins
of wild geese returning to the north signalled the end of winter,
his dreams began to include the old woman. He had entered
the chapel one morning to find her naked and, from that
moment, the image fused with memories of his wife in these
erotic visions. Sometimes he imagined the old woman lying
naked in his bed, her flat breasts like dripped tallow and her
belly dry and wrinkled, and was disturbed to find that he
could be aroused by the fantasy. Indeed he began to enjoy the
idea so much that he started to plan ways of lying with her
without his gaolers learning of it. At other times he was
shocked by his obsession and found the concept completely
repugnant but, as the sun moved daily further north and the
seabirds fought for nesting space on the cliffs, the vision
returned with increasing frequency and with greater intensity
on each occasion.

He lost interest in his currach and used trivial excuses to

linger in the chapel or remain in her company in the evening. He watched her moulding dough for bannocks, the bones in her hands rippling under a frail fabric of skin and knotted veins. He watched her pick sorrel to flavour the water, rolling it sensuously in her long fingers above the bowl. Eventually, unable to contain his passion, he decided to remain in the chapel one evening. She did not seem to be perturbed when he sat by the door and waited for his gaolers to appear. It was Cathair who came to fetch him but, when he saw MacLaine sitting on the stone floor, he seemed to know what was happening.

'You are staying here tonight, then?' he asked.

MacLaine nodded, staring at his feet.

Cathair said nothing but reached down and touched the older man's head. MacLaine looked up, expecting to see a coarse grin but discovered instead an expression of extraordinary melancholy.

'God give you good night,' the young man whispered as he left the chapel.

The woman uncovered her head, combed out her long, white hair and crossed the floor to take MacLaine's hands in hers.

'Come, my lord, we are not children. I know why you are here.'

MacLaine sat for some time after she spoke, his fingers trembling between his knees. She leaned back and tried to pull him to his feet but he refused to move. She took him by the beard and gently shook his head. He looked up and found her smiling. Suddenly he pulled her roughly against him, searching for the hem of her gown. Her skin was surprisingly soft and supple under his hand. As he rolled over, however, she struggled free and stood over him.

'I am too old for a stone floor,' she gasped, offering her hands to him again.

As he rose, she removed his jerkin, leaving only the saffron smock, and slipped her gown over her head. She stood naked before him as he had imagined in his fantasies, her spent breasts hanging from her ribs, her belly, though marked with child-bearing, flat and firm and her long legs well shaped. He moved her towards the heather bed but, as he bent over her, he remembered how Domhnull had touched Cathair in the same room and hesitated, struck by the contrast between the warrior's gentleness and his impetuous assault on the woman. The thought did not dowse his passion, however, and he forced himself upon her clumsily like a youth in his first court-ship, breathless, trembling and uncouth. Her cry rang round the chapel.

Later he lay on his back, gazing at the thatch, ashamed of his lust, appalled by his brutality and disgusted by the whole affair. He rose and, lifting his jerkin from the floor, fled from the room.

Once outside, he leaned against the stone wall and gazed at the stars. The sky was so infinite and clean and he felt sullied and small. Surely he would be punished for his iniquity.

'O Mary, pure Holy Maid, Shrine of Our Lord's Flesh, Casket of Mysteries, pray for my sins . . .' he muttered.

But there was no priest to give him absolution or set his penance and, even if there had been an holy man on the island, he could not have confessed. It occurred to him that he might never see a priest again and might die there unfor-given. That was his punishment, he decided, to be imprisoned on the island for the rest of his life chained to the dreadful memory of that night in the chapel. He peered through the moonless night towards the holy island, hoping to glean some solace from its shadow but it was indistinguishable from the dark cloud on the horizon. He considered returning to the chapel to plead forgiveness but remained against the wall till cold and fatigue drove him back to his quarters.

He still carried water for the old woman and broke her fire-wood but he could not talk with her. When the lythe returned to the rocks he brought her a huge, red fish but he spent most days searching for wood for the currach. By mid-summer, when the sun set in a blazing dome behind Coll, he had made a frame, which he concealed in the rocks.

One morning, as he spread the cowhide on the stones, a pebble fell from the cliff above. Throwing the skin back into the crevice, he looked up to see a figure on the plateau. He could not identify the person against the sun till he shaded his eyes. With great relief he discovered that it was the old woman.

'A small galley for a chief,' she called. 'I must speak with you, MacLaine.'

Covering the hide properly, he made his way back towards the western gateway. She came to meet him on the shore.

'So you are making a currach?'

He nodded, annoyed that he had allowed his work to be discovered.

'You would leave before you see your child?'

'I have no children and, if I had they would not send them here.'

'You will have a child before Yule, MacLaine, and here on the island.'

He searched her grey eyes for meaning, dismissing the immediate conclusion that she had conceived. She was too old. She had been sent to him for that reason – so that he could not leave an heir – but, when he saw her coy smile, he knew that it was true.

'Yes, I am with child. I can feel it in my breasts.'

He turned away, unable to share her enthusiasm and assailed by the realization that he was trapped. He could not leave her to bear his only heir in the company of the two guards, for he knew that, once his kinsman heard of it, he would have it destroyed. He would have to stay and protect the blood line, issuing, after all, from Somerled and Conn of the Hundred Battles. That was his penance.

'They must not know,' he said, clutching her shoulders. It was the first time he had touched her since he had lain with her in the chapel but he was too concerned for the child to notice it.

'I can conceal my belly but they will hear the cry when it is born. They will know then.'

'We will find a way,' he replied with little conviction.

He thought of building a larger currach but the gulls had destroyed so much of the cowhide that there was scarcely enough for a small craft. The woman would have to travel alone, carrying his heir to his people on Mull, or he would have to kill the guards. He resumed his surveillance of the two men, his interest in their behaviour renewed. He discovered that they shared a bed and that they never wore their quilted battle coats. He had no doubts now about his ability to slice through Cathair's neck. His fantasies had vanished. No longer troubled by the resemblance to his wife or the tender scene in the chapel, he concentrated on planning the warrior's death and that of his companion. Even the moments of longing for his wife had disappeared. He had only one task in mind, that of protecting his heir and the fragile creature who bore him.

He wanted to show the woman kindness but knew that any change in his habits or attitude might arouse suspicion.

Winter came early with cold sleet showers from the southwest which left the tops of the hills white above the rocks. The birlin returned with meal and salt meat and a keg of spirit. This time the crew disembarked and, while MacLaine was locked in his room, they consumed the spirit in an evening of debauchery. Cathair, MacLaine observed through a crack in the door, did not participate but watched the others gloomily, obviously resenting their presence on the island. Domhnull, on the other hand, sang and shouted and spilled his drink in the fire where it ignited with a muffled explosion, much to the amusement of the seamen. He hammered on MacLaine's door and invited him to the chapel.

'Come, MacLaine,' he roared, 'let us pray in the chapel, pray with the Virgin, eh? A virgin no longer, I think. Eh MacLaine?'

MacLaine could tell by their coarse laughter that they knew of his night with the old woman. Their crude comments annoyed him but their ignorance of the unexpected result brought him some comfort. Indeed he was quite pleased when he considered how he had thwarted his kinsman by producing an heir to claim the lands which the latter held by force rather than title. Since he had learned of the conception, his perception of the affair had altered. He was no longer appalled by his action and his sense of guilt had diminished. At times he felt quite proud of his achievement but the vulgar remarks of the sailors reminded him of his brutality. He was glad to hear them depart the following day.

By Martinmas the currach was complete. It was an exceedingly small and fragile craft. When he tried it in the creek, it sank almost to the gunwales with his weight but it did float and, on a calm day, he was sure that it would carry him or the woman to Mull. He persuaded his guards to let him have a stave from the spirit keg, telling them that he wished to carve a cross for the chapel but, in fact, intending to make a paddle for the currach.

One evening, as MacLaine emerged for his habitual visit to the well before retiring, he stopped suddenly, astonished by the intensity of the fire in the sky which flickered and rippled from one horizon to the other like the banners of an invisible host on its way to battle. It was overwhelming, inexplicable. Something appalling, he decided, was bound to follow such a display of supernatural energy. He crossed himself in the name of the Trinity and continued on his way.

When he returned, Cathair was standing at the door with a blazing ember above his head.

'The cailleach has sent for you.'

MacLaine tried to appear disinterested but knew that the time of her delivery had arrived. He walked away slowly towards the chapel.

That night, as the sky burned with cold fire, he delivered a daughter, placing the slimy infant on the old woman's belly. The arrival of a female child, a possibility he had never really considered, upset all his plans but, just as he was considering leaving the mother and her child and using the currach to escape himself, the spasms recommenced and she produced a second child, this one a male. Quickly he picked up the lamp and passed it three times sunwise in the name of the Trinity round the trio to keep them from harm but the boy-child cried and, within minutes, Cathair and Domhnull hurried in with their swords drawn.

The old woman, in the meantime, had concealed one of the children beneath the blanket.

'Light the beacon, Domhnull!' Cathair commanded with an air of authority which MacLaine had not heard before. Domhnull hurried back to their quarters, rolled out a keg of pitch, which had been concealed beneath a tarpaulin, and set it alight. In less than a minute flames curled into the sky, illuminating the small window of the chapel. MacLaine wondered how he had missed the keg in their room and cursed his failure to consider that they might have such a signal.

A boat arrived before dawn to carry news of the birth back to his adversary. Obviously they had kept a constant watch on the island from the shore.

MacLaine studied Cathair, trying to detect any sign of wonder or compassion when he glanced at the child, but, quite clearly, he found it repugnant and, when his gaze returned to meet his own, he smiled malevolently and shook his head. He had guessed MacLaine's thoughts.

'Take the Chief away, Cathair,' the cailleach pleaded, her sudden intervention surprising the two men, 'His presence offends me. He cringes under your blade like a whipped hound. Take him to his cell. I do not want him here. Do not worry about me, I will not be moving. I am tethered to his child.'

Cathair was obviously puzzled by her request but stepped back and signalled to MacLaine to comply with it. Once again he was locked in his room.

When the boat returned, it carried an extra passenger. MacLaine could just see his back as he followed Domhnull into the chapel but was unable to identify him. The old woman, however, recognized him immediately as one of the Mull physicians.

'We do not need you here,' she said, clutching one of the children to her breast.

'It will take more milk than you can make, cailleach, to feed the child. I have been sent to see that you are both well.'

He had a kind face with soft blue eyes almost invisible beneath profuse, white brows.

'Go, Domhnull,' he said to the guard without looking round. 'Leave us. This is no place for a sword.'

His voice too was gentle and she began to feel safe in his

company as Domhnull left awkwardly, closing the door behind him. Yet her instincts warned her to distrust the man.

'She is a beautiful child,' he murmured as he stepped forward to touch its cheek. 'It is a daughter, is it not?'

She succumbed to his flattery and began to feel proud of her achievement as she studied its minute but perfectly formed finger nails. She remembered her first daughter, now held as ransom for her services to MacLaine and her husband who had been slain among the newly-turned rigs, the bere seed still in his hand, when the Islesmen had landed. Her memories and the relief following the stress of labour lulled her into a warm euphoria.

'You have tied her cord, I hope?' the physician interrupted her reminiscences.

'Yes, yes,' she lied. She had bitten through it hastily and squeezed it with her fingers.

'Let me see.'

She studied his eyes. They were like the smoke hanging over the hearthstone in her father's house. She remembered the old man's skill with the bow and the ease with which he could bend it to the string. She tried to recall her mother's face but it eluded her. It was a long time ago and she was very tired.

As the physician gently lifted the child from her arms, she knew that she would not see it again. She closed her eyes and listened as he moved towards the door.

'Let her feel the warmth of the sun on her skin,' he crooned. 'The Christ fire on her eyes. Show her to the Earth Mother, her youngest flower, her fairest yet . . .'

She hoped that the child would not cry out when they killed it.

They allowed MacLaine out once the boat had left and told him that the child had been taken to a wet-nurse on Mull. Cathair obviously did not expect him to believe the story and conveyed it with a cruel lack of conviction. MacLaine asked to see the old woman but Cathair laughed at him.

'She does not wish to see you.'

The old woman, however, was longing for his company as

she tried to smother the cries of the other child and to comfort him with what little milk she had. When the men brought her sowens, she held her hand over his mouth.

'Let me see MacLaine,' she asked Domhnull finally, 'I want to tell him how it feels to bear a child and have it torn from the breast before it has a name. Another man's child would still be in my arms.'

They relented and allowed MacLaine to see her.

'I have saved your heir, MacLaine,' she announced when they were alone, 'but I cannot feed him for long and they will soon hear him cry.'

MacLaine nodded as he considered their predicament. The solution was obvious but he hesitated, knowing that the currach could carry only one of them. He did not want to be left on the island. He had remembered where he and Domhnull had met before and the memory gave him every reason to leave. He could still see Domhnull fleeing from his village when the MacLaines had crossed the marches and the arrow meant for the retreating warrior pinning the man's child to the ground. Domhnull might recall the occasion at any time. The image, however, reminded him of what they would do to his son, if he was discovered. His heir, he decided finally, had to be saved.

'Take the currach,' he said finally. 'It is frail but the only hope.'

The chapel shielded them from the guardhouse as they crept down to the shore. He helped her and the child into the craft, handed her the wooden cross to use as a paddle and pushed her out to sea.

'Christ keep you in his care, MacLaine, you are a great chief,' she whispered and kissed him on the brow.

As she paddled the currach out of the creek, he returned to the plateau and watched the tiny craft, like a black bubble, drifting eastward towards Mull. He sat in his seat and followed it till it faded into the moonless night. He looked up at the stars, blinking to clear his eyes, and spoke to the bright light above the holy island.

'Sweet Mary, Mother of Christ, Queen of the seas, pray for them.'

He was overwhelmed with inexpressible loneliness and sorrow. He might never see his son again and he had sacrificed his only method of escape. The next day would be Yule and the sun would begin its long journey back to the north. The fires would not be smoored on the hearthstones on Mull that night and the candles would burn long after cock-crow. Even his kinsman would observe the traditions. He remembered the smell of burning juniper and could still see his wife laughing with the others through the tears caused by its smoke. For a moment their eyes had met and, for those few seconds, the material world had melted away, suspending them together in an infinite and vibrant equilibrium. He fixed his eyes again on the brightest star, trying to recreate that moment, hoping that, wherever she was, she would recall it too . . . but a cloud moved across the sky and he remembered where he was.

USSR

Alexander McCall Smith

As he entered the hallway, he saw that somebody had stuck a small poster on the wall. It was a page of an exercise book, ripped out and stuck up in haste. Paper aged so quickly here, etched yellow by the acid air. He peered at the neat, Cyrillic script, now barely legible: '*Don't forget!*' it read. '*Don't forget who ordered the construction of the White Canal! Don't forget who sent the millions to their death in the camps! The Party has never acknowledged its guilt, never once.*' And beneath, in another hand, somebody had written: '*It has. It did. They're different men now. You don't blame a son for what his father did, do you?*' Then, in another, ill-tutored hand, a bitter, local complaint, a remark which he could not understand.

There were many such posters now – stuck up in the underpasses that led to the metro, pinned to the sides of booths, tacked on to trees. It revealed the living of a political life in the interstices of the system, which was still shy about blossoming into overt dissent. It was everywhere in Moscow, like weeds peeping through concrete, irrepressible.

He looked again at his notebook. It was on the fourth floor; apartment number eight. He was a few minutes late, but that would be expected. To arrive early would be regarded as an eccentricity; even to fail to arrive at all would be accepted, or at least understood. But he could not miss this appointment, which was one of the main reasons for his trip. It had not been easy to arrange, and now that he was here he felt that the prize could so easily be snatched away from him. He could be lying dead inside the apartment; he might be five, ten minutes too late. Or he could have changed his mind. He might be silent, or accusing; he knew these people could be like that, particularly if they still believed.

Now he stood before the door. There was no name on it,

but the number was right, and so he pressed the bell. Nothing. He stood for a moment, recovering his breath from the climb up the stairs, then he put his thumb against the button and pressed again.

'It's you.'

'Yes.'

The door opened wide and the man inside gestured for him to enter. The smell, he thought; that smell that you find nowhere else. What was it? It had been explained to him as being the smell of cheap Soviet soap, the smell carried by people in their multitudes on the Moscow subway, understandable there, with so many bodies; but here?

'Come through. Come through. We can sit in the living room.'

They crossed a small passageway and went into a room which was plainly furnished – chairs, a knotted rug from some Asian republic, an electric samovar. He looked about him, fascinated. It was so hard to get invited to a Russian house – it hardly ever happened, even now. Yet this, of course, was not a real Russian house – it was a Scottish house, in a way; an unusual Scottish house.

He looked about the walls. One of them was totally covered with framed photographs of the sort sometimes to be seen in the houses of the old. There were photographs of groups, of meetings, of men shaking hands, of a woman, of a profile, of a man with medals laughing at something.

'My icons,' the man said, and then laughed. 'Every one of them.'

There was Dundee in his voice still, and the young man thought: this is incongruous; but why? He remembered the film he had seen of the other sort of exile, the fashionable, arty traitor, drawling in the accents of the thirties drawing room or the Oxbridge college, talking of their contemporaries as if we all knew them, or should still be interested. That did not seem strange, perhaps, because one heard so much of it. The English loved their handful of class traitors, their homosexual spies. But nobody heard anything of this man, who was honest, and never betrayed any cause he served.

He fetched tea, served in glasses in small silver stands.

'I can't offer you coffee,' he said. 'I haven't seen it for weeks.'

'I'm sorry. I could have brought you some. I didn't think . . .'

'That I would take it?' He laughed. 'Son, I'll take anything. I'm not proud. Why should you be proud about a present?'

The 'son' came out so easily, and once again he thought of the street where he knew this man had been born, and of the community in which he had grown up, and of how all that had gone.

'I saw what you wrote about me,' the older man said. 'I read your piece in *The Herald*. Good. It was good. And now you want to write more?'

There was somebody else in the flat, somewhere in another room. There was a noise, a sound of human movement. He had expected him to be living by himself after the death of his wife, but perhaps not. Nobody lived alone in Moscow; there were people everywhere, crammed into every space. He had seen the refugees sitting hopelessly outside tents pitched on waste ground, uprooted, hungry, the victims of long-nurtured hatreds, hating.

'I hoped to ask you more about your life here,' he explained. 'I know all about the bit in Scotland, and the time you spent in Prague, but then nobody knows much about the years you spent here in Moscow.'

'You could look in the history books. It's all there. Not about me, of course, but about Moscow, about Russia. I just lived through it – that's all.'

He was puzzled.

'I don't quite understand.'

His host laughed. 'All I'm saying is that I was just part of everything that was happening in the . . . in the bigger world. I worked in the House of Friendship and did some books for Progress Publishers, and for the rest I experienced and felt what every other Soviet citizen was experiencing and feeling. I've never been one of the big people.'

He raised the glass of tea to his lips and took a sip. It could end up in platitudes. He might be tight-lipped; he might tell him nothing. He might spew out the Marxist stock phrases of the past, and nothing more. After all, what was he asking of him – to recant the past – to say it was all a mistake?

'Don't get me wrong. I'm not saying that it hasn't been interesting. I'm not saying that I haven't had a good life here and done the things that I want to do. I'm not saying that.'

They talked for an hour. Fresh tea was served, and small, white biscuits, which tasted of almonds. Then the older man got up, stretched, and looked out of the window.

'It's awful tiring talking about your own life, you know.' He scratched his head and hitched up his trousers. 'We could go for a walk. The river's not far away. Would you like that?'

'I would. And then . . .' he paused. 'I wondered if you would let me take you for a meal.'

He looked surprised. 'Where? You know it's difficult to get into a restaurant in Moscow. You can't just turn up. This isn't Edinburgh.'

'I know that. I booked days ago, through a Russian friend. I got a table at a place which is not too far away and which is very good.'

The older man looked at his watch. 'Thank you. Yes, I'd like that. We could go for our walk and then I could meet you there later on, when it's time.'

They walked slowly, on the pavement next to the river wall. There were holes in the paving and they had to navigate their way round these; cracks; holes; gaps where the concrete had caved in. And everywhere, on every pitted, crumbling surface, there was a layer of dirt. There was dirt on the window ledges of buildings, on the parapets; on the leaves of the trees; dust and dirt, dirt.

He said: 'You can't imagine how strange it was for me at first, when I came here all those years ago. Look – I didn't speak any Russian, none. But they put me in a course, free, and they hammered away at it and in six months I had the language under my belt. Then they gave me a job and somewhere to live and, later on, my citizenship.

'That was my proudest moment. There was a ceremony

and the local secretary gave me my badge of citizenship. Then my friends took me to get drunk with them somewhere out near Zagorsk, in somebody's place out there.

'I used to get so many letters from home. People wrote to me as if I'd changed into some sort of . . . some sort of new creature or something. They wrote to me with bated breath, as it were, in stilted language, and asked all sorts of daft questions which I couldn't really be bothered to answer.

'I know what you're thinking now. You don't really have to tell me. You're thinking: what does he make of it now that it's all crumbling? Well, I'll tell you: it's not over, not at all. We may have our difficulties here – all right, all right – but we built a decent society that believed in the health and the schooling of bairns and in spreading what there was about fairly. Why can't people accept that? Is that anything to be ashamed about?'

They walked past two young men, standing beside the river wall. He saw that they were deep in conversation and that one seemed on the brink of tears. Their voices were lowered, and one was emphasizing a point by moving his hand up and down in chopping motion. And he thought: the one nearest the wall is objecting to military service, like so many others – he won't serve – the militia have a warrant for his arrest and the other is trying to advise him. In such a society, where is there to go?

Suddenly something within him seemed to rise up against everything that his companion was saying. Ever since he had arrived in Moscow he had felt a dull sense of hopelessness, an emptiness that he had never felt or experienced anywhere else before; not on the dying streets of Maputo, nor in the shanty town of Bogota where his breath had been taken away by the reeking brick works with their child labourers. Here in Moscow he had seen it on the faces of people on the street; on the faces of those in the queues; on the face of the girl he had seen in the bleak, echoing shop as she moved empty boxes under an empty red star. Nothing. Three generations of effort come to naught.

He wanted to turn to the man beside him and say: 'What is it like to believe in God and then find that God is finally, definitively proved not to exist, not to be there? What do you do?'

But then he thought: 'You can't say that to a man of sixty-five who has given up his life to his cause.' He would have said it five or six years ago, when he was younger, and believed in hurting people to make a point, but not now.

So he said instead: 'I wonder what this Georgian restaurant's going to be like? I'm told it's good.'

At the restaurant, they were served course after course, in the Georgian style. There was liquor, too. Vodka to go with the red roe and lemon and then dark red wine, dry and strong. They talked as they ate, about the people he had met, of his travels. He had gone to virtually every corner of the Soviet Union, lecturing, talking. His descriptions were vivid, off-beat.

He wanted again to say: 'But surely the place is falling apart. Look at it. Nothing works. Material needs aren't satisfied. It's finished.'

But once again he didn't; he just ordered another bottle of wine, and they filled their glasses once more. Then, at the end, the waiters began to look at their watches and he called for the bill. It seemed pathetically cheap, but he knew that it was a week's salary, perhaps more.

The waiter shook his head and whispered.

'Dollars.'

'What?'

'You must give me dollars, or pounds. Pay that way. No roubles. No.'

He glanced across at his guest, who was looking at the waiter, his eyes glazed. Had he heard?

'I don't want to pay in pounds,' he said softly. 'I'll pay you in roubles.'

The waiter's eyes narrowed. 'Cheat,' he said. 'When they booked the table they said you'd pay in hard currency. They promised.'

He thought quickly. Had they? They had said that they would have to bargain to get the table – is that what they meant? In which case, he thought, he would have to pay that way, although he knew that the money would be siphoned off, that it would never get as far as the cashier. This wasn't officially a hard currency place.

He reached into his wallet and took out several banknotes, which he folded and put down on the small tray which the waiter held in his hand. The Queen looked back at him from the notes. They got up and left the restaurant, fussed over by the waiters. Good night. Good night.

And then, out in the Moscow street, they walked slowly back to the metro station. The older man was silent. Then he said: 'I heard that. I saw it.'

He replied: 'I had to do it. My friends must have promised a bribe, promised foreign currency. You know how it is here.'

The other turned his head away, as if ashamed. His voice was quiet, cracked, like an old man's voice telling of some great, painful loss.

'I do,' he said. 'I know.'

And the young man would have put his arm around him and comforted him, and said that it did not matter and that perhaps it would come right, that there would be an end, or a new beginning, or whatever; but they were near the station now and the moment had passed and he sensed that there was no time for comfort before the train came.

IN THE CITY
Esther Woolfson

She began walking before dawn, before the light had begun
to rise slowly from the direction of Wadi Ahba. When it did
begin, it was a thin line which spread and grew till the sky
was grey and she could see the glint of straight, smooth blue
which was the road.

She walked slowly over the stones, one hand supporting the
child, the other holding their bundle of things. The child had
fed early in the darkness of her husband's parents' house,
poorly as it always fed and because she had not watched it
feed, she thought that today, it had taken more. She thought
that every morning. It was a belief which shrivelled towards
evening and died before renewing itself afresh each morning.
The sky lightened as she walked till she could see the traffic
beginning on the road, one car going south, after a few
moments another and then a silent line of heavy trucks passing
north.

From the moment of his birth, the child needed nothing. When
the midwife drew him out, he seemed not to need to breathe.
She had quickly stopped his anus until he gasped his lungs
full but even at that moment, he did not cry. He seemed
not to need food and sucked reluctantly, taking in little and
dribbling out all but the tiny quantity which kept him alive.
He was born small and stayed small, a thin monkey of an
infant with long toes which curled under and long white
fingers which he moved slowly, touching and stroking at
things in the air which no one else could see.

His mother Zeinab, whose first child he was, was too full
of her own joy in his birth to notice, for the first few days, his
silence and stillness and the way he did not seem to need her.
She let the other women look after him until she recovered.

She did not hear them talking as they rubbed his wrinkled, reddish body with salt and oil.

'This one doesn't belong to anyone. I've seen them like it before,' the midwife said, taking his long foot in her hand. The women all whispered to each other that he did not want to live – but he did live, sucking weakly, vomiting, retaining just enough to keep his eyes opening, his hands moving slowly to catch at the light or at the moon glowing through the window or the down which floated in, exploded from the dry, ripe thistles.

'We are in the midst of war and death,' his grandmother murmured between her prayers at the moment of his birth. She knew that there are not always explanations for why some words from among all possible ones flood into the mind and that these were the ones her mind had chosen to greet the joyous event of the birth of a boy. That evening, she thanked God although she did not know what she was thanking him for. Forty years before, she had rejoiced over the birth of her first son.

This son, whose birth had been met by feasting and the firing of rifles into the sky, Hamid, the child's father, was given permission to come home from the army in the west to see the child. He left the ruined streets of the foreign city where he was serving, full of pride and new, profound delight, travelling home with his knowledge of himself as the father of a son changing the familiar into the unnameable and beautiful, his happiness making him sing in the truck which took him half his journey. On the bus which took him the rest of the way, he felt that his joy would last for the whole of his life.

Even before he saw his son, Hamid knew that he had rejoiced alone and for the last time. People in the village went quiet when they saw him, melting away behind houses, drawing silently into doorways, the women covering their faces and turning away. Looking into the child's face, he saw its thinness, its pallor and its look of unending resignation. When he picked the baby up, Hamid felt its weightlessness and knew that he was holding something which had been there, but which had gone. His heart, which had seemed large with his pride, turned and folded small as he stroked the baby's head which was covered with a haze of fine black hair. He watched the child sleep and feed and lie staring and when he travelled back west, he realized he had not heard him cry. He wondered if the joy he had felt had ever been and whether his wanton, unquestioning foolishness in feeling such joy could ever be erased, the hole its having made in him being deeper than a wound which would at least close and heal over in time.

In the village, people had many explanations for the way the child was. Some of the women felt that his mother was too old, some his father, while many believed that it lay in the union of the two. There were those who believed it to be connected with his mother's having been married twice, the first time widowed.

An elderly woman called by everyone Khadije the Stranger because she had come from the south as a girl, brought Zeinab a charm for the child, a frog made of silver on a plaited red cord which she tied round the baby's forehead. After Khadije had left, Zeinab untied the frog from the baby's head to look at it. Its edges were worn smooth and Zeinab felt its age must give it power. It shone, making Zeinab think of stars as she dangled it on the end of its cord in the sunlight in front of the child who followed the sparkling arc it made with his wide, grey eyes. When he stopped watching it, she tied it carefully round his forehead again.

People in the village remembered Zeinab's dead husband for the first time in years. A small, quiet, ugly man not unlike Hamid, he had died long before in war. They counted back over the years he had lain, his body never returned for burial. They thought too about the desolate plain where he had died and about his skeleton. They knew that uniforms rot more slowly than flesh. They thought about how bones whiten and empty, about the sand which covers them and the way wind blows the sand away.

He should have been returned, many people now said to one another, wondering if there was any connection between this and the child's illness.

By the time she reached the road, the sky was light enough for Zeinab to look back and see quite clearly, the village, the walls which for decades had been crumbling without repair, containing or failing to contain, the spill of square, ochre houses, minarets, towers which rose undifferentiated from the stretch of flat ochre stone and earth and dust she had crossed. She sat down on the edge of the road to wait for the buses which began to pass from first light, stopping she had been told, if there was room, carrying on if there was not, across the light, vast stretch of land to the capital in the south.

Zeinab eased the cloth that tied the child to her. She stroked his head and sang a song to him that her father had sung to her, about a nightingale. The note for the doctor was in the front of her dress with her money and the money her father in law had given her, saying it was for the boy, his eyes filling, beginning to drip a succession of large, slow drips down the folds between his nose and chin as he said it. The note with the name of the hospital at the top, was addressed to a doctor whose name no one could read. It had been looked at by most of the people in the village but they found the quick, flat writing, the abbreviations and the interspersing of words they recognized with those they did not, impossible. It was only a few words and, disappointingly, told them nothing. Only Abu Zuheir had commented, taking the paper, shaking his jowls which bristled with half-shaven whiskers. He told the women that the words, perfectly well understood by him, were too secret and important to be divulged to them.

'Only for the doctor! Only him! Not for you!' he said, and he took his knowledge and his halting, upright dignity out into the lane while the women laughed, knowing that Abu Zuheir had read the letter with his one stone-like, opaque and sightless eye. Zeinab saw that 'possibly' could be made out and 'quickly' but she soon put the note away, not needing a letter to tell her what she knew.

As Zeinab saw a bus approach, she stopped singing about the nightingale and stood up to wait for the bulky, grey shape to stop. Blurred, moon-like faces in a row looked at her from the windows as a man helped her climb the three, deep steps.

'Here! Sit here!' An elderly woman with a scattering of blue tattoo marks across her face moved closer to the window,

169

pulling her black dress round her to make room for Zeinab on the seat. She leaned towards Zeinab as she settled in the narrow space and hissed onions and bread and garlic into Zeinab's face.

'Where is it you're going?' The woman gripped Zeinab's forearm with a hand of iron.

'Is it to visit your mother? Your sister? Where is your husband? Ill? The child? Oh, oh, let me see!' She tugged the covering away from the baby's head to peer down on his veined, quivering eyelids and white sleeping face.

'He's so pale!' and the old woman put one hand over her mouth while with the other, she fingered a loop of blue beads pinned to the front of her dress.

'God will decide,' she said, 'it is in the hands of God.'

Outside, deep orange light lit the line of the horizon as the sun rose to its place in the blue, clearing sky.

'I would take him quickly,' the doctor said looking at Zeinab, the doctor with the yellow skin and tired eyes which to Zeinab were the eyes of all women. Cold spilled down into Zeinab's chest as the doctor said it, her eyes saying too, take him quickly. In the village, people who came back from the town said that townspeople never smile but Zeinab knew this woman did smile, but not now, saying with her tired eyes, take him quickly, the skin falling into little cracks and folds around her eyes. Zeinab did not say, is it because I am too old? She did not ask but wondered if, had she been younger, her child would have guzzled and flailed and screamed like the other babies whose mothers moved quietly away from her in the queue which formed beside the clinic van.

'Zeinab, you now,' they urged, pushing her forward in the line for the doctor, wishing her and her sickly child gone, trying to put as much space as they could between Zeinab's child and their own whose fat, shining arms would be pierced soon by the vaccination needles.

'I'll give you a note to take to the hospital,' the doctor said, 'give it to them when you get there,' and she wrote words on a piece of paper. There is no medicine, Zeinab knew as she watched the yellow hand write the quick, flat writing, that is

170

more powerful than the will of God. She wanted to ask if she would have more children and why she had waited so long for this one, but she did not ask, for no word, even that of a doctor, could challenge the will of God.

'Take this to the hospital,' the doctor said, 'and they will do what they can for your child.' She handed Zeinab the note which she took, saying her thanks and saying too, 'It is in the hands of God,' at which the doctor looked down but did not reply.

After half an hour, Zeinab had travelled further south than she had ever travelled before. She had been north but never south to the capital. She thought, leaning back in the cramped seat, feeling the child's weight shift slightly against her, of the journey she had made with her father once when she was a child. They had travelled to see their family village for the last time before it was covered by the lake which was to be created by the construction of a vast, new dam. The village was empty when they arrived, their people having already been moved to a raw, half-built town far away from the dam site.

Zeinab looked past the old woman, out at the quiet plain. She remembered the silence of their visit, the stillness, the sadness as they walked through the house where her father had grown up, out onto the white, glistening salt marshes which, her father had told her, lifted in sheets when the wind blew from the south, to fall back down like a shroud over the village. She remembered the river whose water was to drown the land, flowing green and slow and sluggish, like a somnolent snake through high, sand banks. Of the new town where her family lived, she remembered only that the sky was strangely narrow, too narrow, a long, transverse strip of blue showing between the tops of buildings so that when she thought of towns, she thought of floating shreds of torn blue.

Zeinab dreamed after the visit to her father's village, of drowning. She wakened her sisters crying and clutching at their hair. Their grandmother took Zeinab one day to collect the honey from the hives. She gave her a piece of comb to suck and told her that, at her age, girls often dream.

The bus stopped to pick up and drop passengers. There

was little room now and people settled themselves on the floor. When someone got off, everyone craned to watch them begin across the open plain. Herds of camels grazed and men on donkeys passed across the flat country, shimmering now under a haze of moving light.

In the growing heat of the mid-morning, the bus stopped at a small town, turning off the main road and through the streets to the bus station. The passengers dispersed to buy tea and bags of melon and sunflower seeds and sweet cakes. Sitting on the platform, Zeinab fed the baby who was awake but silent. With a cloth, she wiped his face and sopped up the white fluid which leaked from the side of his flaccid mouth.

'So, that's it, eh?' The old woman came up behind Zeinab and watched, squatting by her, leaning over her shoulder, 'No wonder he's a stick!'

She thrust into Zeinab's hand a pastry she had bought for her and sat to eat her own with her few, flashing gold teeth.

'Eat it, come on, eat it,' the woman urged, 'it'll put him right,' and spluttering with laughter, she sprayed the air around with pale flecks of food and spit, her tattoos disappearing into creases of wrinkled, brown skin. Zeinab ate the cake slowly, her throat closing to meet it. When she had finished it, she put her hot, sugary fingers into the baby's mouth and felt the cool ring of flesh close round them, and felt him suck feebly at each one in turn.

The morning passed on the line of blue tarmac, turning into noon as they entered the city which began slowly, like the few drops of rain which become a torrent. A few shacks, a half finished house or two, a pile of canvas awning, then low buildings which became higher, broader as the streets grew broader, blocks of flats, dusty shops with half-lowered metal grilles. Then there were wide streets lined with trees, high, fine buildings, iron balconies, areas of garden, flowering trees, water sprinklers which turned slowly over grass. Cars did not pass in thin, metal lines but jostled as ants jostle in the carcass of a chicken, dark and voracious. Squares of glass glinted the colours of sun and rainbows. Zeinab leaned over the old woman to look out in wonder at shop windows, packed and brilliant, cavernous entrances to huge buildings, banks, offices, flights of steps where people from a different world walked. And indeed, there above her, she could see the narrow sky like a river of blue edged with roofs and aerials, washing lines flapping through leaves which filtered sunlight on to pale, splashed pavements, ragged strips of sky which hung too low in the dense, amber air.

As she stepped down from the bus, Zeinab's arm was caught by the old woman in the swirl of dust and people outside. Sun and dust half closed Zeinab's eyes against the surroundings, the press of booths selling drinks, lottery tickets, magazines, trestles of platters piled with heaps of cakes and sweet biscuits, bread stands, upright spits of meat watched over by men with long knives, cafés whose smeared windows held huge bulbous jars of red and purple pickles floating in brilliant, luminous liquid.

'Come, I'll show you where to go. The hospital's out of the city, on the road south. You must find the road and go on, on, on.'

Zeinab shook the old woman's hand from her arm and turned away from her, stepping carefully to avoid the full, flowing gutters. She held the hem of her dress up, away from the brown water, the puddles of dark mud oiled with spreading flowers of green and blue and purple, the dead, stiff rats floating sodden in the drains. People rushed, pushing as they went, boys with trays of bread balanced sturdily on their heads, men whose blinking, swishing donkeys needed the whole width of the streets to pass with their loads. She eased into the crowd. The doctor had told her that the hospital was in the centre of the city. Moving out carefully into the current of the street, Zeinab was wary, watching for people who might approach her or think she was easy to steal from or detain. She knew that she was among other people who did not know the way, people looking for buses to take them somewhere, people looking for relatives or friends, among soldiers, children, beggars. She walked out into the full noise of the street, cars, radios, music, engines and voices tangling into an urgent, acrid din which rose above the mud and benzine and sugar smell of the streets.

The day closed round Zeinab as she carried the child through the crowded streets and markets, through small courtyards where women hung washing and children played round open doorways, through squares which opened into further, quieter squares where tall, balconied houses of golden stones seemed to catch the hush and hold it in the dim, enclosed space. In the darkness of the covered market, she passed through pools of dusty sunlight let in by the tears in the broken iron roof. She walked past women shopping, buying from piles of bright fruit and gleaming vegetables, fingering and sniffing, selecting from long racks standing in the street, searching among rows of shoes and dresses, hurrying to fill days of which Zeinab knew nothing. She knew only that these were the days lived by other women.

Men sat in caverns of cool, flickering light under stone arches, drinking coffee and smoking under the fans which rotated slowly from low ceilings. As Zeinab passed into the street of meat traders, flies rose at her, falling from black, hanging heads dripping above her, crawling over her hair and down into the baby's ears and round his head. She brushed them away and turned back, away from the street, round a corner where she stood for a moment watching a boy measure a clear, sweet perfume from a large bottle into a row of small ones lined on the counter before she went on, into the street where cloth was sold, full of muffled sound and the sour smell of cotton. Stall keepers called to her for the first time, urging her to buy, pushing bales towards her, their stripes and checks taking her eye. Headcloths, black and white and red hanging from poles, coloured scarves like flowers blowing gently in gusts of warm air.

One stall holder moved out, a thin, wolfish man with a white cap and dark, straggled beard circling her, standing momentarily in her way, urging her in a low voice, 'Come, come look,' making clicking noises with his tongue. She walked quickly past him, trying not to look into his narrow face and wolf's eyes. He was gone by the time she turned into a dark street lit by hissing soda lamps but she looked back once or twice to make sure he had not followed her into this dim place where old men sat in open shop fronts mending watches and bicycles, cutting keys, clanging hammers, showering blue sparks from blue flame. Parts of greasy, blackened metal lay on stained cobbles under string loops which supported wheels, springs, harnesses from the vaults. In a corner, Zeinab laid her bundle down and rearranged the child more comfortably round her. A man behind her clanged a flat iron down on a furnace before taking it up and with his bare foot, skimming the hot, black iron over the steaming, brilliant white surface he was ironing.

No one addressed her except the cloth sellers. As she walked, Zeinab felt as if her life had begun that very morning, like a birth without memory. She could not remember any other life, not the village, her family or her husband. She felt as if her life had been crushed underfoot like a beetle's casing, crushed by the life of the city. Men and women who possessed familiar lives and memories and knowledge rushed past her so easily that she might have been invisible, a spirit which did not exist in the world of men.

She put her hand to the baby's cheek and under his nose to make sure his breathing was still coming. It was, shallow and damp and even. Bending to him, there was nothing in the dust-filled darkness of the street except herself and the child, bound steadily, inseparably, by the will of God.

Passing beyond the markets and dark streets, Zeinab walked out into the bright light. Sounds of children's voices reached her from behind a high wall. A jasmine growing inside the wall had climbed to the top and now fell, a cloud of green and white, along its length. Zeinab stopped and picked a stem, sniffed its perfume then held the white star flowers under the child's nose. Following a sign on the opposite wall which indicated with the depiction of a pointing finger, the way to the great mosque, Zeinab walked on, into the colonnaded courtyard. Worshippers gathered, passing in and out of the huge doorway, into the interior of the mosque where she longed to go but could not, being unclean still after the child's birth.

A woman in a black coat with a white scarf tied tightly round her fat and smiling face, rose from her chair inside the mosque's gate and led Zeinab to where a group of women sat on the polished mosaic of the courtyard. Zeinab sat and drank the water the woman had poured for her from the flask under her chair and listened to the conversation of the other women, where they came from and why they were there, their children, their husbands, their errands in the city. Zeinab did not say why she was there. Slapping the baby's face lightly to wake him, she fed him and washed his face with the water she had left in the bottom of the glass, dipping her cloth in, uncurling his hot fingers and wiping his palms free of the tight rolls of black fibres gathered from her dress. Rising, Zeinab hesitated, but then did not ask the way to the hospital.

When Zeinab did ask, it was of a woman who was coming out of a house, still talking to someone inside the doorway. She was being pulled vigorously by a small boy in the brown smock of an elementary school. He was tugging at her hand, dancing on the spot in his impatience.

'It's not far,' the woman said, adjusting her spectacles over her pale, protruding eyes to read the note Zeinab had shown her. She led Zeinab to the corner better to show her the way.

'Is it for you?' the woman asked shyly.

'No, for the baby.'

Zeinab watched the woman's eyes protrude more, her face flush as she looked at Zeinab, imagining her own son ill, thin, dying. The boy had now begun to clamour and whine.

'It is in the hands of God,' she said, putting her hand on Zeinab's arm and letting her heavy lids drop over her big, round eyes.

'It is in the hands of God,' Zeinab repeated, watching as the woman was swiftly propelled out of sight.

'Soon. We will be there soon,' she whispered to the baby, who slept on.

The rhythm of the day is the same everywhere and Zeinab at last began to know the rhythm of this day which wearied her in the quiet lull of afternoon. The sounds of the street were muted in the heavy, orange heat. Only the sounds of voices, dishes clattering inside houses and water running let her know that some things about people's lives are the same everywhere. She felt her strength soaking into the hard, stone pavements.

Opening beyond a patch of empty, stony ground, the narrow street gave way to a wide boulevard as the woman had said it would. Zeinab crossed between the cars and along by the low wall as she had been told until she reached the long, high building with the lawn and the trees and the high metal gate which the woman had described. The notice board held the same name as the piece of paper. Looking up, Zeinab could no longer see the sun which was burned to a dull, indistinct haze of brightness in a heavy, ashen sky. The water sprinklers moved in their slow circles over the grass and bright flowers, catching Zeinab's hand as she walked towards the steps. The emptiness and quiet of the hospital seemed full of faint, dying echoes of doors closing and voices speaking.

A young woman sat at a counter behind a glass partition. She was reading a magazine which she continued to do for some time after Zeinab had entered. After a time she lowered the magazine and looked at Zeinab who was whispering to the child, 'We are here, we are here.'

'Yes?'

Zeinab handed her the note and watched her face as she took the grubby, finger-stained paper, marked by the hands of the many people who had simply wanted to know. Her red lip curled slightly and she handed back the note, holding it by a corner.

'He won't be back till six.'

'Six?'

'Yes,' she said impatiently, 'that's what I said. Six. He'll be back at six. Come back then.'

The young woman propped the magazine up against the glass of the partition. On its cover there was a woman with blonde hair and naked shoulders. The young woman began to pick her teeth with a small wooden stick.

The water from the sprinklers was being blown sideways as Zeinab walked down the path, through the fine spray which wet her dress at the knees. She had not thought that he might not be there. She had carried his indecipherable name around with her constantly and now, he was not there. Disconsolate, she felt tired and hungry, and thought suddenly about the roasting meat and sesame bread in the market. As she crossed the boulevard to retrace her steps to the market, the wind blew a hot gust which unsteadied her and left a film of dust in her mouth. She drew the cloth up closer over the child and looking up, she knew that she was somewhere she had not been before, not heading towards the market at all. She could see a line of high, sand-coloured hills, the city flowing over, climbing the hills in long fingers. Hamid, she whispered wishing he was there, wishing to share her fear, to end being alone with it, wishing to have Hamid go as she could not, into the great mosque where he could kneel on the sea of carpets rich with the smell of sweat and feet so that in there, he could implore God to turn his will.

Hamid, in his city in the west, was circling slowly with other men in a half-track around a bulldozed lot where two standing walls and a shattered staircase provided a nest for snipers, empty that hot, damp afternoon. Hamid thought of his son and began to cry, cursing, spitting out his curse over the moving metal edge of the vehicle, cursing the people of this city who killed so easily and with so much apparent pleasure, other men's sons.

In the vast square, Zeinab was caught by the fear which seemed to travel on the gusts of wind which began to fill the air with fragments of grit, blown newspapers, sand and fine dust. The square was crowded and filled with the sound of people hissing, pressing, pushing, trampling as the wind gusted, cutting the square from corner to corner.

The wind which blew most summers rose as if from nowhere, dropping down from the still heat on to the city. The wind rose in the south, gaining strength in the rise and fall of heat over the desert. It came, some people believed, as a result of God's anger, sudden and righteous, from the broad plains eaten by salt and sun which lay silent, deep, benign until the soft air began to lift golden sand against the wind. Clouds ringed with burning dust blew pillars of sweeping stone particles screaming down around the hill-encircled city.

The square was filled suddenly with dust and blue, moving light which diffused and flickered, broken by the sweep of dust as the wind blew through the crowd which groaned and swayed and moaned. The crowd itself seemed to blow, fluid, moving, grey, a ghost's army of white, moving figures, heads and faces covered against the dust, against the growing darkness. Zeinab was too slow, blinded by the sweep of salt and dust and sand which filled her eyes while hands pulled and bodies pushed and moved and grappled past her and round her, on into the shrieking curtain of yellow, horizontal wind. She could not move; her nose filled too so that she could not breathe and felt herself drowning, gasping in the acid dust, turning from the storm which screamed once more across the square and died, leaving a shocking stillness when people stood momentarily before scuttling away, bent like crabs or scorpions across the square where Zeinab still stood in a small, clear space and knew as she felt in front of her, her eyes fighting to open, that her hands were empty and the child gone.

Biographical Notes

ELIZABETH BURNS lives in Edinburgh. Her poetry has been published in various magazines and anthologies. 'Visitors' is her second story to be published in this annual collection.

GORDON BURNSIDE was born in 1944. He grew up in and lives in Dundee, where he has done a variety of jobs. His play *A Man at Yir Back* was performed at Dundee Rep in 1989 and 1990 and at Glasgow's Mayfest. A one act play *Jumbe, or Millions o'Mince* was performed at the Scottish Student Drama Festival, Glasgow in 1990. 'Pass the Parcel' is his first published story.

MERCEDES CLARASO was born in Glasgow in 1924, of a Scottish mother and a Catalan father. Her childhood was spent in Spain but she has lived in Scotland for most of her adult life. She has been involved in library work, in school and university teaching and has run a wholefoods shop.

ERIK COUTTS lives in Lincolnshire. 'Tsantsa' is his third story to be published in this annual collection.

ROBERT DODDS was born in 1955. He read English at Oxford, and has worked as a teacher and lecturer in England, Mexico and the USA. He is married with two children, and now lives in Edinburgh, where he is lecturer in film and video production at Edinburgh College of Art.

ALLAN MITCHELL FOWLIE was born in Montrose in 1955. He was brought up on the east coast of Scotland, in Kenya and the West Midlands, and now works as an assistant film editor for the BBC in London. 'Scum of the Earth' is his second story to be published in this annual collection. He and his wife Doreen have a daughter.

RONALD FRAME was born in 1953 in Glasgow, and educated there and at Oxford. His most recent novels are *Penelope's Hat* (1989), shortlisted for the McVitie's Prize and the James Tait Black Memorial Prize, and *Bluette* (1990). A new novel, *Underwood and After*, will be published in 1991.

JANICE GALLOWAY was born in Ayrshire. She has worked in a variety of paid and unpaid jobs but has mostly been a teacher. She now makes her living from writing and reviewing music. Her short stories have been widely published in magazines and anthologies. Her first novel *The Trick is to Keep Breathing* was published in 1989 and a collection of short stories, *Blood*, followed in 1990. She likes cities and lives in Glasgow.

JOHN HERDMAN was born in Edinburgh in 1941, and educated in Edinburgh and at Cambridge. Some of his fiction was collected as *Three Novellas* (1987); his other books include a study of Bob Dylan's lyrics, *Voice Without Restraint* (1982), and *The Double in Nineteenth-Century Fiction* (1990). He is a former Creative Writing Fellow at Edinburgh University.

IAN MCGINNESS was born in Glasgow in 1954. He is married and has worked in Scotland and Ireland as a teacher and as a farmer. Two of his novels have been published by Polygon: *Inner City* (1987) and *Bannock* (1990). He currently lives in Glasgow.

CANDIA MCWILLIAM was born in Edinburgh in 1955. She is author of two novels *A Case of Knives* (1988) and *A Little Stranger* (1989). She lives in Oxford.

CHRISTINA MILLS was born in Glasgow. She is a poet and the mother of two grown-up daughters. She has collaborated in amateur theatre productions and is a partner in her family business. Currently, she is a student at the Open University.

DEBORAH MOFFATT is an American who has lived in Scotland since 1982. Her stories have appeared in a number of periodicals and anthologies, including *The Listener*, *Cosmopolitan*, *Critical Quarterly*, Faber's *First Fictions* and Bloomsbury's *Soho Square*.

WILLIAM OLIPHANT was born in Glasgow in 1920. He left school at fourteen and worked until he was sixty-five in a variety of jobs to do with the servicing of radios, televisions and, finally, electronic keyboard instruments. He began writing poetry in 1983 and has had poems published in *Chapman*, and poems and stories (including 'Bearsden Bagatelle') in *West Coast Magazine*.

WILLIE ORR was born in Northern Ireland in 1940, leaving the province in 1959 to work as a hill shepherd in the Western Highlands of Scotland until 1974. He attended Stirling and Strathclyde Universities as a mature student and now lives in Argyll, writing and teaching. 'A Child at Yule' is his third story to appear in this annual collection.

ALEXANDER MCCALL SMITH was born in Zimbabwe in 1948 and educated there and in Scotland. He is the author of over twenty books, many of them for children. He lives in Edinburgh.

BIOGRAPHICAL NOTES

ESTHER WOOLFSON was born and brought up in Glasgow. She was educated at the Hebrew University of Jerusalem and Edinburgh University. She has worked as a translator and a journalist. 'In the City' is her second story to be published in this annual collection.